Tonino Guerra

Equilibrium

–

Translated by Eric Mosbacher

With a New Introduction by Michael Bracewell

Published in 2020 by Moist
https://moistbooks.cargo.site

Original Italian edition first published in 1967 as *L'Equilibrio*
by Casa Ed. Valentino Bompani & C., Milan
© Casa Ed. Valentino Bompani & C., Milan

First English Language translation published by Chatto &
Windus Ltd, in 1969, now republished in the UK with
permission of Andrea Guerra

Introduction © Michael Bracewell 2020

ISBN 978-1-913430-01-6
eBook ISBN 978-1-913430-00-9

A catalogue record for this book is available from the British
Library

Such is the gravitational field of legend that it is difficult to approach Tonino Guerra's fiction without thinking of his screen-writing associations with Fellini, Visconti and Tarkovsky. His novel 'Equilibrium,' first published in 1967, lies squarely between the visionary, historical and Neo-realistic tendencies that the films of these great directors share.

Character, situation, destiny and psychological landscape have a cinematic aura in Guerra's novel. Time, place and event acquire their own psychological independence, becoming autonomous narrators in their own right. (A similarity with Tarkovsky's film masterpiece 'Stalker' and in more comic mode the films of Jacques Rivette.)

At the same time, Guerra's use of language ("I caught a glimpse of a V-2 passing low over the treetops, lurching through the grey air like a rusty old lorry." for example) combines concision and intimacy with compelling energy. His prose is suspenseful, driven by apprehension as much as a cartoon-like sense of the absurd or deadpan.

Guerra's subject is the experience and memory of wartime imprisonment in relation to the post-war acceleration of 'modernity'. Endings and beginnings are blurred and vertiginous. Progress is accosted by unexpected events; the narrator's comprehension of how he reached a certain point is assailed by paranoia and impetuous assumptions. In the world of 'Equilibrium' there is no equilibrium: everything past and present tilts and slides – nothing matches or correlates; episodes and events, however neatly or even casually related, appear to crash into and through their respective places in time.

'Equilibrium' is an account of a mind unravelling in its attempt to understand itself. Its owner is drawn ever-deeper into a maze of beliefs, activities, recollections and perceptions that are prompted and shaped by his experiences in a German concentration camp towards the end of World War Two. The present becomes an increasingly detached sequence of problems, confrontations, tests and delusional epiphanies.

Our narrator is an anonymous male graphic designer from Milan. He stresses that he is a quintessentially modern being. His world is one of services and products: Coca-Cola, Alitalia airways, sectional kitchens. But he begins by declaring his desire to leave this 'urban' world; and does so by acquiring a house in the country 'by correspondence' – receiving even the keys in the post, in a cardboard box.

You could liken this transition to the moment in Fellini's film 'City of Women' when Snaporaz (an urbane Lothario played by Fellini's on-screen alter ego, Marcello Mastroianni) alights from an express train in the middle of nowhere in order to pursue an apparently alluring woman.

From the moment he leaves the train, Snaporaz has stepped through the looking glass into a world that will answer only to its own logic. Similarly, once away from Milan – the 'urban' to which 'Equilibrium's narrator had been tethered - past and present overlap and meaning, interpretation and communication must be reconfigured.

His predicament is both existential and semi-comically related to design. His destiny is steady withdrawal from society – fascinated by rubbish in the streets, surprised that it has been thrown away.

The encounters and experiences within this temporal labyrinth become a mystery that the narrator is simultaneously creating and attempting to solve. The commonplace becomes weighted with significance. As Alice discovers in Wonderland, one illogical situation leads only to another, infuriatingly bound to its own illogicality.

And it is with Alice-like suddenness and non-sense that the originating trauma of the narrator's hectically racing experience is introduced out of nowhere: "Talking of cabbages, I shall never forget the camp commandant (as S.S. officer aged about sixteen) …"

Thus commences the central narrative, detailing the imprisonment, intimidation, abuse and murder of a group of prisoners. The inference is that this wartime story has broken free of its temporal boundaries to haunt the narrator. A principal attribute of this short novel becomes its constant interrogation of its own world. In this lie both its narrative momentum and the neurotically pedantic mindset of its 'voice'.

Readers coming new to 'Equilibrium' might be reminded in places of the earlier, analytically quotidian novels of Nicholson Baker: a phenomenological approach to description that in turn opens portals to new courses of action, insight and assumption. Guerra's extended disquisitions on the nature of stones, Swedish matches, lettering, symbols, canes and lines all stem from commonplace or potentially 'reasonable' circumstances.

Their subsequent illogicality is both immediate (like the light coming in a refrigerator when its door is opened) and slippery – having the appearance of necessity, sense or reason. All, in one way or another, comprise a gnomic semantic search for language and legibility; yet all are equally unknowable, equally illegible – and intentionally, anarchically so. (Anarchy being the opposite of equilibrium.)

"They were condensed symbols that got into your blood" – says the narrator, as he excitedly conceives of a new form of lettering that is "fragmented, sectionalized" like kitchen units - "and haunted you until they expanded in your mind, revealing the content of the message. That was the theory. It was an anti-clarity, anti-easy reading, anti-speed, anti-the-whole-of-modern-life-theory."

From the outset, this modern narrator treats his 'anti' situation as a series of interrelating mysteries and puzzles, the temper of which combines the narrative complexity of film noir, the episodic, parable aspect of visionary journeying (such as one finds in 'Pilgrim's Progress' or an early song by Bob Dylan) and a darkly absurdist half-comedy in which the narrator, Chaplin-like, becomes the stooge of either fate or his own mishandling of his affairs.

'Equilibrium's modernist literary precursors are more Russian than Italian. Most notably the narrative voice of Andrei Bely's novel

'Petersburg' (1913) and even more so that of Benedict Erofeev's samizdat novella, 'Moscow Circles', written and first circulated around 1970. Both novels might be termed absurdist, entropic and as tragedies. The narrative voice of both is likewise questioning of its own experience and in part comically so.

In such vein Guerra's narrator questions the hereness of here, the thingness of things and the nowness of now – an occupation common to both twentieth century philosophy and post-war countercultural thinking. He holds his perception of his own traumatic history and existence up to the light, like a child minutely examining a curious object.

This examination prompts him to construct systems and analyses that may be linguistic yet expedite his drift into a world of deceptions, doubles, paranoia, hallucination and madness. All stemming from and leading irrevocably back to the horrors – the quasi surrealist madness – of the prison camp, its prisoners, punishments, commandant and deaths. At the same time, the narrator tells his story in a manner that is often conversational and impassively unquestioning of the associative jumps and swerves that always return to his nightmarish memories.

To summarise the story of a novel that pits itself against story-telling – or claims to – is entirely in keeping with the illogicality and conundrums by which it is also defined. In 'Equilibrium' we find the traumatised, reactive, restless attempt of late modernism to understand the individual in relation to history and existential crisis. American equivalents could include the fiction of Thomas Pynchon or Kathy Acker and films 'The Swimmer' and 'Repo Man'.

There is an appealingly punkish edge to the narrator's mix of assertiveness and flippancy. Readers will find his voice and story linger – become sympathetic, usefully disruptive.

"I am perfectly capable of making long and perfectly lucid speeches, but that bores me; I prefer talking as the spirit moves me, saying whatever comes into my head." And he adds, for good measure, "But if I go on telling everything in order I shall start feeling sick."

Michael Bracewell, 2020

Equilibrium

Equilibrium

Contents

I might become a bore myself,
for instance,
if I were not one already.

18

I had just got away from it all, by which I mean all those ordinary, boring things like skyscrapers, cigar-smoking industrialists, linoleum, plastics, television, westerns and marihuana. I had either seen or heard about them. Whether they are good or bad is beside the point. All I am saying is that that was the world I had come from, the urban world. And when one has said that one has said everything. I haven't mentioned anything about myself yet, but my personal description is as follows: height, five foot seven, age forty-five, thin, an ordinary man, in fact. Occupation, graphic designer. I've done a great many things, packaging, advertising campaigns, scent bottles, a new design for a packet of British cigarettes, the trade mark for Cornell safes and the house emblem for a patent medicine firm. Incidentally, I have also been to Chicago, and I once met Gropius. I even had a letter from him, which I kept. Married, but no children.

I am the sort of person who hates explaining. I need to be understood in a flash. I am perfectly capable of making long and perfectly lucid speeches, but that bores me; I prefer talking as the spirit moves me, saying whatever comes into my head. Otherwise it's an effort. And besides, it's not worth while. That is an important point, a very important point indeed: it's simply not worth while. If I held my head in my hands and tried telling you everything in minute detail, I haven't the slightest doubt I should succeed. I see everything quite clearly, including the precise moment of my arrival at the house in the country, what I was carrying, and how I walked all around and looked at it before going in. Also the stony riverbed right in front of it. But if I go on telling everything in order I shall start feeling sick.

Arriving somewhere and having the feeling that you have been there before is an experience that everyone has had, that's an old story. But what happened this time was even more extraordinary, because when I got out of the Volkswagen and started walking round the house I knew for certain that I was coming to a big wooden door, with cracks covered with rusty tin, and there it was, just as I expected. I was completely taken aback, because how can you possibly have such details in your head if you have never been to a place before and not even seen photographs of it? There were some things that did not coincide with the house I had in mind, of course. Some of the walls and rooms were different, and there were some cracks. But, broadly speaking, it was as I remembered it. I must of course explain that I had never been in that part of the world before. I had bought the house because the news that it was for sale got as far as Milan. A station-master mentioned it to his daughter, who mentioned it to a client of mine, who happened to mention it to me. So I decided to buy it. On the spur of the moment, just like that. The whole thing was done by correspondence.

Even the keys were sent to me in Milan in a cardboard box. No, not in a cardboard box, those were some other keys. I can't remember what they were now. Actually someone either brought them to me or left them downstairs with the hall porter. Not only did I buy the house without seeing it, but I never had the pleasure of meeting the vendor. Incidentally, I think I sent money to an intermediary, so I never discovered who the owner was. Somehow I have a feeling that he had gone to America, and that there was a complicated story about a legacy behind it. So much for the house. The same applies to the whole area. I mean, I had never been to that part of the world before. The areas of Italy I know, apart from Lombard plain down as far as the Po, are the Tyrrhenian coast and regions of the type of Tuscany, Latium and Calabria, let us say; though I have never actually been to Calabria. But this area I didn't know at all. I knew that Ancona, Apulia and the Romagna existed, but only as hearsay, and this house was in the Adriatic area, between the Romagna and the Marche. So it was impossible that I should ever have seen it in the course of my travels. I realize that I have always kept to the west, not only in Italy, but also in Europe and the rest of the world. There is a meridian I have never crossed, I think it's the one that runs through Bologna, Hamburg, Norway, the North Pole, etc.

There was of course another possible explanation. Thinking about imaginary houses in the country had always been a habit of mine, and I used to do a great deal of it it in Germany. Taking refuge in an imaginary house in the country was a way to escape from that hell; and I felt quite sure that anything you had made up or imagined must really exist somewhere or other.

At any rate, those were my first thoughts after my arrival. Immediately afterwards, as soon as I started arranging my luggage and things in the big, empty rooms, a kind of frenzy got hold of me. To me traveling is always a highly dramatic business. Let me give you an example. In 1964 I went to London, Savoy Hotel, room No. 853. The trouble began at Milan airport. I always get to airports and stations an hour early, so as to allow plenty of time to go home and fetch whatever it is I'm sure to have forgotten. A very necessary precaution, because there's always something or other I have to go back for. But this time I checked through my suitcase and could find nothing missing. All the same, I had the feeling that something was missing. During the flight I reassured myself with the thought that whatever it was that I had forgotten would reveal itself at any moment. Actually I could not wait for the revelation. But it did not come. In the taxi from the airport to London it was the same. I was so preoccupied by this that I didn't see the landscape. By landscape I mean traffic signals. I had long since ceased noticing grass or trees. To a graphic designer the landscape consists of arrows, signs, advertisements, traffic lights. Anyway, I got to the

Savoy. I went to my room, opened my bags, had a bath, put my comb, perfume, toothpaste and hair lotion in the bathroom. I looked for a toothpick, and actually found one. But I went on striding restlessly around the room, feeling sure I had forgotten something. Later on, in the West End, in the shops at the *Queen* office and back again at the hotel, it was the same. The whole time half my mind was working away on its own account, worrying about whatever it was that I'd forgotten. And of course I went on kicking myself for my own carelessness. But after twenty-four hours I calmed down. I could not have forgotten anything. In fact I was sure of it. But, so far from being comforted, I found this disconcerting. I wondered whether I had changed, degenerated into a precise and careful fellow, particularly as London, with its swarms of young people so unrestrained in every way, with their clothes and hair and everything, it made me feel more bourgeois than ever, something of a white-collar worker, in fact. That was why I had found my disorganized way of traveling so comforting. At least I had had that. But now I had deteriorated. Improvement always involves deterioration, that I knew. So I had the disagreeable feeling that I had changed. Fortunately, when I got to London airport on the way back, I could not find my passport. I had left it at the hotel. That reconciled me to myself again. I don't know whether I really forgot it or forget it on purpose. On the other hand of course, when you loose or forget something, it's a sign that you want to lose or forget.

At the house however, the problem of having forgotten something did not arise. I had packed hurriedly, putting in a bit of everything, wanting to have little or nothing, particularly as far as clothes were concerned. In fact I had very little. Only one pair of shoes for instance: the pair I was wearing.

The only furniture that had been left was a big, black wardrobe, a kind of huge beetle with two curls on top that looked like feelers. It was in the bedroom already. Or rather it was in the room in which I put my camp-bed because it was there. Otherwise I left the room empty. I put my two suitcases in the middle of another room and left them there, so that when I wanted to change I had to take things straight from a suitcase. So the wardrobe stayed empty. The only precaution I took was to keep it locked, to prevent anyone from hiding inside. I always think about burglars, murderers and bandits. There were two holes in the wardrobe. A bit of metal was sticking out of one of them, a bomb or shell fragment that had ended up there when the front passed this way. The wardrobe was a skeleton, nothing but an air container. When you struck it with your fists it was very sonorous, because the wood was as hard as bone. The curls reached up nearly to the ceiling. When you looked at it by candlelight the whole wardrobe seemed to move forward as if it were staggering. After locking it on the first day I opened it again only once, and let out a hornet that had been imprisoned inside, or perhaps it had been born there and was trying to come out. After it came out I tried shutting myself inside. I stayed in the dark for an hour or two. When I came out it was night-time. I tiptoed over to the bed and flung myself on it as if I were attacking someone. I grabbed the pillow and crushed it between my fingers until I had throttled it.

Bedrooms are very important. There are some in which you know at once you will be able to sleep, and others in which you know you won't be able to bat an eyelid. I have slept in many bedrooms, and few have been right. But now I know what a bedroom has to be like. It has to be small, with a rectangular glass window and heavy wooden shutters. The bed must be low, to save you having to make sure no one is hiding underneath. The door must be in the wall towards which your feet are pointing, so that, if an intruder comes in, you'll have time to get up and defend yourself - he'll have to cross the whole room before grabbing you by the throat, whether he's a ghost or a murderer. The most convenient form of a bedside table is a chair, if possible one of those with a straw seat on which you can put a glass of water, matches, cigarettes, and a candle. You need a candle even if there is electric light. There may be a sudden storm, and if there's an electricity failure you can light the candle and go close the beating shutter. Pictures on the walls are disturbing, and there should be none. A bedroom is intended to be dark. Thirty cubic meters of darkness.

* * * * *

I had to design some new lettering for Snaidero Sectional Kitchens. This is why I had gone away to the country. Designing new lettering nowadays is not easy. After the enormous vogue of Cairoli during the past ten years, Haas, which was nothing but the old Helvetica revised and brought up-to-date with some romantic flourishes, came in, but now it's on the way out, and we are moving towards bold - that's as certain as *The Times* will be coming out tomorrow morning. Among other things, you have to think of characters with a very condensed face, and if, for instance, you have three characters T, L and P all in the same word, you're in trouble, because there's too much air around them, while there's too little round others, which form smudges over-crowded with pothooks. The problem is to invent a lettering in harmony with the age. Max Bill may have shown us the way; the lettering he used for a magazine title looks as if it had been designed by a computer, and its multitude of articulations and compact zones reminded one of short circuits.

Those were the lines on which my mind worked during the first few days. I painted a big T, an L and a P on a strip of cardboard, diminishing the horizontal stroke of the T, the foot of the L and the loop of the P so that there should not be so much air around them, with a view to giving them a compactness more in keeping with the other letters. But, having improved the spacing, I had doubts about the clarity. So I redesigned them, lining them to give them greater strength, painted them red, and took them for a long walk to the river-bed. At a hundred yards' distance they stood out quite plainly, and at two hundred yards they did the same. I planted them in the ground on a sandy flat and, to make sure they were still easily legible at speed, got on a lorry that was loading gravel, and asked the driver to step on the gas and drive past them. Also I laid them flat on the ground, to make sure they were suitable for use in horizontal publicity. They survived the test. Next I designed a lower case *i* with a square dot, to suggest a punctuation system based on the square. I hung the four letters on the wall of the big ground-floor room, and sat on my haunches and looked at them.

Then I started wondering what on earth this T, P, L and lower case *i* had to do with my coming to the country. You cannot possibly begin to design a new lettering single-handed, you need a whole team, seven or eight persons working together for at least a year. Some different and more ancient necessity must have driven me to this spot. I knew I had come here because I had to, but I could not remember when or where the compulsion had begun to grow inside me. At all events, I felt fine. I started taking short walks along the riverbed, backwards and forwards without rhyme or reason, looking about me, and that was all.

Until I picked up a blue stone. I noticed it in an expanse of dusty, whitish stones. I was struck by the strangeness of its color. I thought I had found the only blue stone in the riverbed, and that was why I wetted it with spittle and rubbed it clean in the palm of my hand. Then, strolling back towards the house, I found another, and another, and then a great many more. They were all of slightly differing shades of blue. I arranged the on the brick floor of one of the many empty rooms. They looked very good indeed. That night I went to bed thinking about them. Next day I went back to the riverbed to collect all the blue stones I could lay my hands on. A deep red, almost chestnut, stone caught my eye, and I picked it up, and I also started picking up all the red stones I could find. Eventually I decided to collect stones of any attractive color, including white, particularly the milky-white ones that are used in making lime and cement. By the time I had finished I had taken several loads of stones back to the house and laid them out on the brick floor. At 10 p.m. that evening I stood and looked at them by candlelight.

Next day I took a fancy to stones with lines on them. White lines forming regular circles, or irregular lines that started somewhere and zigzagged round like petrified little flashes of lightening. Also there were stones with patches on them, grey stones with a green stripe in the middle or green ones with a grey stripe. But after two or three days my interest in colored or curiously patterned stones evaporated. Suddenly I noticed there were stones of extraordinary shape, like feet or ears, and others that looked like plants or animals and all sorts of other things. So I started looking for stones of that kind.

My first find was a shoe. A greenish, stone shoe. It had everything, the sole, the shape of the tope, the opening for the foot, and even some twisted white lines that suggested laces. A little farther on there was a slab with the imprint of a naked, human foot. I took off my shoe and sock and put my foot on it, and it fitted perfectly. So that day I made two finds. Next morning I found an eye, and some stones shaped exactly like bones. I covered the floor of another room with that sort of thing. One afternoon I discovered a stone exactly like a dog's head. So much so that it revolted me, and I dropped it. After that my sympathies extended solely to stones that were more stone-like than others, so stone-like, in fact, that they couldn't possibly be anything but stones.

I took the Volkswagen and went off to look for a telephone to call up a man I know in Milan who is a publicity genius. It was he who came up with the slogan: He who buys a car buys himself. 'What can be done about selling stones?' I shouted down the receiver. He shouted too. Our conversation was as follows:

X. - The only trouble is that there's a vast supply.

Myself. - That's not necessarily the decisive factor. People manage to sell earth, after all. I mean earth, in sacks. It may be good earth, but still it's earth.

X. - Perhaps the target should be the collectors' market, and the slogan should be: YOU COLLECT STONES. WE FIND THEM FOR YOU. But the trouble with that is that collectors like making their own discoveries.

Myself. - But there are collectors who by collections ready made.

X. - What's worrying me is the woman shopper. To my mind she's the real snag. I can't imagine a woman going into a shop and asking for 5 lb. of stones. That's what you're up against.

Myself. - They could be packaged like Baratti sweets, or wrapped in tissue-paper like oranges. But we're certainly up against the problem of weight; 8 lb. of stones are too heavy for a shopping basket.

X. - But don't forget, nowadays coke is put up in bags for easy transport, in 56 lb. bags, I think.

Myself. - No woman in the world will ever be persuaded to carry 56 lb. bags of anything.

X. - Of course not, but there could be a home delivery service, with discounts for large quantities.

Myself. - And special offers.

X. - Certainly. There would be no transport difficulties in flat country, and in the mountains they could easily be solved. Distribution presents no problem, but the question remains: Why should women buy stones?

Myself. - Supposing we tried a different approach. Supposing we tackled it from the tourist angle. Why not a campaign to send people to see stones? There are the mountains and the seaside, and they could be sent to any amount of other places to which they otherwise wouldn't want to go. They could be sent to them to see the stones. In other words, the aim would be not so much to sell stones as the sight of them.

X. - You would have to be specific. The mountains are full of stones, there are far too many. You would have to say: Go and see the stones of the River Such-and-such or So-and-so for the following reasons. That way you might get somewhere.

Myself. - Or we might promote a kind of Japanese garden, with paths made of nothing but stones. Set a new fashion. Beautify your garden with stones.

X. - I disagree. But one might launch a campaign for the protection of the stones of our riverbeds. A campaign, with enormous headlines, to make it illegal to collect stones from them. We could announce that the ravages caused by collectors were doing irreparable damage. The reaction would be a desire to possess stones, and so you could create a market for them.

Myself. - Yes, that's sound enough, but first of all we must create a desire for beautification by means of stones.

X. - Certainly.

Myself. - What's your idea of the cost of a pound of stones?

X. - It would be quite high, if you ask me. At first sight you might think that they would cost nothing but, when you come to consider the matter, it's obvious that a great deal of expense would be involved. They would have to be collected, cleaned and packaged, and then there's the problem of selection; for that you'd need a conveyer belt system, and of course a staff of women workers to do the selecting.

Myself. - Would you call them stones or rocks?

X. - The word 'stone' is humbler, more popular; 'rock' is more aristocratic, I might say even precious, and it has sharp and jagged edges, it implies a sense of danger which is absent from the word 'stone'. 'Stone' is rounder, friendlier, it's easier to hold in your hand, so to speak.

Next day I took all the stones I had collected and dumped them back in the riverbed.

Whenever I'm drowning,
for instance,
I forget to shout for help.

Talking of cabbages, I shall never forget the one the camp commandment (an S.S. officer aged about sixteen) held in his arm that evening as if it were a baby in swaddling clothes. It was a bluish cabbage, with big, twisted leaves. All the cabbages he held in his arm every evening and every morning were like that. With the other arm, at the end of which there was a steel hook instead of a hand, he detached the leaves one at a time and handed them out to the prisoners lined up in front of the hut. He inserted the hook in the lower part of the leaf near the stem, where it was thicker, tore it out and handed it to one of us. On that first evening this cabbage leaf ritual made a big impact on me. I held it in my hand like a fan. Everyone else did the same. Then, when he ordered us to eat, we began munching like rabbits, starting at the top of the leaf, where it was more tender, and working right down to the white, which tasted much more bitter. All the other prisoners were strangers to me, and the camp was still strange to me too. I had just arrived, in a motorcycle combination driven by a sergeant who had picked me up behind the front. There was a rotting wooden hut, a red villa which was the camp headquarters, and a yard of black ashes with remnants of wood and metal among them as if something or other had been burnt, and barbed wire all round.

Afterwards they explained to me that the cabbage was part of a punishment. The object was to find the prisoner who had stolen the commandant's watch, the commandant being the sixteen-year-old S.S. officer with a hook instead of a hand. The real punishment was something else. Every night at nine, or ten, or midnight, or whenever he felt like it, he was going to come into the hut and fire three shots in the dark. Three revolver shots. He was going to start that night. If there was anyone who had nothing whatever to do with all this, it was obviously myself. Even the officer had seen that I had just arrived in the side-car. So I asked to be allowed to sleep somewhere else. But the answer was no.

Incidentally, I had had an appalling day as I had come straight from the front, where I had been digging slit trenches. Ten feet long and five foot eight inches deep. A German arrived with a measuring stick every evening to check that we had done the work correctly. We were in a demolished elementary school which was machine-gunned every day. At two o'clock that morning, or it may have been three, the earth started trembling. The concrete floor began to shake, swell and crack. I rummaged for an old tin in which I had boiled a vest to kill the lice, and went off with it in the dark. I found a path through the wood, and struck my head against a pile of shells, and then against some tree-trunks. I caught a glimpse of a V-2 passing low over the tree-tops, lurching through the grey air like a rusty old lorry. I reached the edge of the wood and came out into a plain that was beginning to be lit by a murky dawn. The air was full of hot metal fragments that came from heaven knows where and went whizzing into the soft ground. There was also a wind, an unnatural wind, that sent all the paper that was lying about, old newspapers, letters, stamps, straw, and feathers, whirling into the air. And there was I in the middle of it. But one can get used to anything, and I ended by listening to the whistle of the shells, foreseeing their trajectory, and managing to dodge them as if they were stones instead of bits of white-hot lead capable of penetrating an iron safe. Black clouds sprang out of the earth, leaving men lying on the grass scorched or with limbs torn off. There were bursts of fire, cries, open mouths, feet stuck in the mud. Weapons were everywhere, and hands, and bodies, and heads tied up with filthy bandages. Clutching the tin in my right hand, I advanced on all fours, to avoid offering a target. I moved my head continually in the metal-laden air. I got to a ditch, and started watching a row of sheep calmly grazing in a steam-bed under the supervision of an old sheep dog which was standing in the middle of the narrow strip that separated the grass of the steam-bed from the newly sprouted corn in the big adjoining field. The sheep looked greedily at the corn, and one of them stretched its head in that direction, but the dog went for it and bit its paw. The dog had clear ideas, as clear as yesterday, even in the middle of the earthquake. That corn must not be touched.

A wheel detached itself from a lorry and ran across the field, tearing up some prickly bushes in its path. I and someone else - I don't know who he was - fell into a pond. I saw his shoes. I got up. He shouted something, and fired at me, but hit the pond three times. I rolled away, and then found myself among some people who were wandering about in tattered clothes, holding their hands to their faces to prevent them being hit by shells. Then I came across an abandoned gun, a lorry lying on its side, two more lorries and a bicycle, and a soldier's hand gripping a bayonet. I crashed into the wall of a house. A house at last. I hunted for the door - anything to get inside four walls for a bit of shelter - found it, and went inside. I went upstairs, and into a kitchen with majolica hanging on the walls and a table with eight plates full of soup that was still warm - the silver spoons were still in it. Where were the people who had been eating it? I sat down and began helping myself, but suddenly there was the sound of footsteps tramping up the stairs, and eight young airmen trooped in, in brown leather trousers and jackets with scarves round their necks. They laughed, and slapped me on the back. They finished their meal and went off, taking me with them down to the road, where three aircraft were hidden by big camouflage nets. They removed the nets. Then they started up, bumped over the uneven ground, and took off into the air that was full of crows' wings and flying bits of lead. A motorcycle with a side-car stopped beside me, and a small, dusty, bespectacled sergeant took me and put me in the side-car. We set out along a track that wandered off into the plain. We moved away from the advancing American tanks, the roar, the fragments exploding from the quivering earth. It took an hour before the noise died away completely. And there we were at the camp where the commandant handed out cabbage leaves.

I had to share the top of a double bunk. The man I shared with was sick. He was the kind of sick man who never stirs. He just lay there all day and all night. I don't know what his illness was, but he was perpetually scratching himself. You could hear the scratching even at night - perhaps it was so audible because there was nothing between the nails and the ribs. Or perhaps he did it on purpose to irritate everyone. During the daytime his hands just dangled. And they were blood-stained. The others slept on sacks of straw that were lying about. There was Violini, an Italian whom the Germans had taken from the prison at Brescia, he was a little man about the size of Victor Emmanuel III, there were some Russians and a few Poles, one of whom was a priest, and a Serbian who slept in a corner of the hut and must once have been as big as an elephant - you could tell by the bones that held up the clothes that covered him; the rest of him was nothing but a lot of terrifying hollows into which the folds in his jacket and trousers subsided. There were also two Czechs, man and wife, who slept underneath me, either belly to belly or back to back.

I don't know how the row with Violini began, but somebody must have begun it. At all events three of four prisoners went for him and wanted to know where he had hidden the watch. As he was a professional thief, it seemed obvious that he must have stolen it. The row started up about ten o'clock, after we had all been lying awake for an hour waiting for the door to open and the officer to come in and fire his three revolver shots. Outside the dogs were roaming about; they were released every night to roam around the camp. Inside it was dark. At first no one had wanted to go to bed. Most of the prisoners thought the best idea was to stand against the wall, because they thought the officer would be bound to fire at the floor. Then we found ourselves packed like sardines in one corner where the elephant man slept. The only one who didn't keep moving about but stayed quiet was the man who was ill. He actually laughed and stopped scratching; the fact that now he wasn't the only one to die, but that everyone else was in the same boat, put him in a good humor. Between one move and the next there were intervals of deep silence while we held our breath, listening to the officer's footsteps, through all we could hear was the dogs padding about. It was during one of these intervals that the Polish priest told us to go down on our knees and pray.

Then everyone started gradually drifting back to his place, his corner, his straw sack, as if to say what will happen will happen, and it was then that the row flared up and the attack on Violini began. It was like lifting the lid of a refuse bin, because Violini was just like a refuse bin. For one thing, his body was covered all over with paper, tied to his waist with string and paperclips, and there were all sorts of other things as well, heaven knows what roguery they were intended for, and he actually had some crusts of bread hidden up his sleeves. His straw sack was full of rubbish that filled the air with dust. All the paper and other stuff was torn to shreds by ten or twenty hands hunting for the watch. At first the things he shouted and yelled were more or less coherent, but they subsided into sharp, mouse-like squeaks. Suddenly, naked as he was, he made a dash for the door and vanished outside. He had gone out of his mind. We heard the dogs get him. It didn't last long, because they knew what to do with escaping prisoners. They went for the throat. Violini had the strength to let out a few yelps, and then the breath left in him was only enough for a whine.

At about midnight, it may have been a little before or a little after, we heard the commandant's footsteps. They grew louder and louder, and stopped just outside the hut. We heard him urinating against the outside of the wooden wall. Then we heard footsteps again, more uncertain this time, as if he couldn't find the door. Then there was a long silence. Then, from the

41

metallic click of his revolver, we realized he had come in and gently closed the door behind him. His alcoholic breath spread through the hut. His revolver was certainly pointing somewhere. I thought about living in a house in the country near a riverbed full of stones and with no water. Being alone in it, without even a dog. Alone with the sun and the shadows. And with my hands in my pockets. The first shot rang out, and we all yelled as if we had been hit. Then there was another silence, and then the second shot rang out, and then the third.

After he walked out we were so exhausted that we dropped off to sleep without a thought for the man who had been killed, or perhaps only wounded. We discovered who it was early the next morning. It was one of the Russians. He had only been hit in the arm, nothing serious really, but he died from loss of blood. He had groped around the room in the dark, dripping blood in the faces of several prisoners, but no one had given him a helping hand. We buried him in the pile of ashes that covered a large part of the camp.

When you fall in love, for instance,
you fall in love with yourself,
but when you commit suicide you kill someone else.

It was by pure chance that I noticed that the field in front of the house formed a green rectangle. I was standing at the window, gazing at the riverbed. The stones looked like animal teeth that had been dropped by chance. One on top of another and one after another. Also there were big holes, full of shadow, in the cracked sand. With one's eyes half closed it was like looking at a piece of blotting paper covered with ink stains. I noticed that the field was rectangular when I happened to lower my eyes. It looked as if the grass had been carefully cut to remove the irregularities all round. Some white lines appeared, and then a big arrow. Graphic designers are liable to that sort of thing; they see signs when there are none. All that is necessary to set them off is catching sight of a rectangular or circular or triangular space. Even the clouds have to look out, particularly cirrus clouds, which are often round, otherwise a letter or sign or the name of some product promptly appears. To the graphic designer not even the moon exists; all he sees is a round object that sets his mind working.

I subjected the grass rectangle to close examination that morning. I carefully paced out its length and breadth; it was exactly thirty-eight paces by fifteen. I looked at it from various angles and distances.

And then, I don't know why, I strolled to the cane-brake behind the house. I moved aside the rustling canes, sat on the ground, and decided to surround the grass rectangle with a cain fence.

I started cutting canes at eight o'clock next morning, and went on until seven in the evening, by which time I had a huge pile, all of exactly the same length, six feet to be precise. Then I fried myself a couple of eggs, flung myself on the bed and went to sleep. Next morning I went on with the job, cleaning canes and laying them in the sun to harden them. I started actually making the fence on the third day. Or perhaps it was the fourth or fifth. First of all I fenced in the whole area, leaving only a small opening on the riverside. Thus it ceased to be a mere two-dimensional space; it acquired volume, a volume of air. During the night I went several times to the middle of the area, where I laid a stone exactly fifteen paces from the fence. I could reach it even in the most complete darkness without counting my footsteps. But that was easy, because I had noticed that there was a slight rise in temperature near the canes, which reflected the warmth. This variation in temperature was perceptible up to midnight, after which it vanished. Then, to reach the canes smoothly and with precision, I had to revert to counting fifteen paces.

Three days later I started making an indefinite number of inter-communicating rhombuses inside the rectangle, forming a kind of labyrinth. Thus the garden began to assume its final shape. I was attracted by the changing play of shadows formed by the sun in its parabolic course, and decided to spend a large part of the day in the rhombus at the end of the labyrinth, lying on the grass along the long line of shadow on the wall.

I went down to the riverbed and collected twelve flat stones, on each of which I painted a number in red paint, beginning with 9 and ending with 20. At nine a.m. I placed stone No. 9 on the line the shadow formed on the grass by the left-hand wall. At ten o'clock I put stone No. 10 on the line of the shadow thrown by the same wall, which was now shorter by about a hand's breath. Similarly I placed stones 11, 12 and 13 at an hour's distance from one another, so that they looked as if they had been dropped there by chance. At one o'clock I had something to eat, and at two o'clock precisely I put stone No. 14 in place on the line of shadow cast by the righthand wall. At eight the job was finished and I had a perfect sundial. I decided not to use my wristwatch any longer and put it in my pocket. When I got up in the morning I could tell the time by looking at the shadow.

I decided to do nothing but just keep still. To look at the canes and do nothing else. It was not easy to realize that I had nothing in front of my eyes but a cane fence. One doesn't see things because the mind is a mechanism in constant conflict with one's eyes. One's

47

eyes try to show one things, but one's mind projects images on them, an infinity of things coming directly from one's childhood. Faces, words, rain, wars. Dream stuff. Totally imaginary dream stuff.

I don't know whether it was five or six days later, or it may have been ten, but one afternoon I heard footsteps. Someone had entered the labyrinth, and was hesitantly advancing towards the last cane rhombus in which I was lying in the shade with my face towards the fence. Out of the corner of one eye I looked at the little entrance. The footsteps on the grass stopped. I tried to make out who it was through the canes, but all I could see was a dark patch, a kind of heavy, opaque shadow. Meanwhile on one of the canes, covered with dry scales, that were right in front of my eyes two huge ants were approaching each other. They were moving their feelers and their bellies were covered in dust. They stopped some distance apart and spent a long time looking at each other. Then one of them moved a feeler, perhaps asking for recognition, or as a sign of friendship. The other did not respond and remained motionless. The first shook its abdomen, but the other stayed still.

The opaque black patch on the other side of the fence approached the fence and obscured the gaps in it. I could hear warm, damp breathing.

'Who is it?'

'It's me, Luisa.'

48

I had completely forgotten that she had arrived. She had said she had come for a few days, or possibly a week, and had made herself a bed somewhere. It was a year since we had slept together, and we hardly spoke. Through the canes I saw that she had undressed and was sunbathing in the middle of her little precinct. I turned my back, leaning against the fence that separated us. The canes were as hot as if they had fever.

I had been married for seven years, but had never seen my wife's breasts. True, I had held them, kissed them, caressed them, but always in the dark. But I had never seen them in the light, I mean in daylight or by electric light. I had often wanted to make love to her with the light on, but she always refused. There were so many things that she refused. Perhaps that was one reason why we stopped making love and she was unfaithful to me. She had an affair with someone that lasted five or six months, and told me about it after it was over. We were living in Rome at that time, because I was doing something or other for the Alitalia airline. Design work, as usual. I think it was the design for the letter-heading, which was repeated on the hostesses' uniforms and on the traveling bags. She did not tell me about it to my face, but wrote me a letter and left for Milan. I found the letter, and the flat was empty, there were just some handkerchiefs lying about, some of them between the cushions on the divan. They were wet, as if she had been weeping. It was four o'clock in the afternoon when I read the letter. I went to see a friend

49

to ask his advice. When I arrived he was playing a game of patience, the kind in which you have ten cards, then nine, then eight, then seven, and so on and so forth. I helped him finish the game. Then I went to see someone else but he was out, and while waiting for him I spent an hour looking at a book on Bisser, who is a very interesting Swiss painter. As my friend didn't come back, I left and wandered about the city. I got as far as the Piazzza Barberini, where I stopped and threw bits of paper into the fountain.

By this time Luisa had taken off her brassière. I spent a long time looking at her firm, white breasts. She was basking like a lizard in the sun. Then a battle between her and the shadow cast by the fence of her enclosure. With the movement of the sun the shadow gradually lengthened, and whenever it reached her she shifted towards the wall on the other side of which I was lying. Suddenly I had the feeling that the shadow was trying to take her, particularly as at one point I noticed that it had covered her completely, perhaps because she had dozed off, and it seemed to be weighing down on her, forming dark patches under her breasts, on her neck, and in the hollow lower down where the darkness was massive and violent. It was at this point that I started talking. Or rather I didn't talk, but called several times, to wake her. Then I said: 'You're in the shade.' And again she moved closer to me in the small remaining patch of sunshine.

By about five o'clock, or it may have been six, the whole of her body was against the cane fence on the other side of which I was lying, and I realized that I wanted her. I was lying on the other side of the fence, with my head exactly level with hers, and my body and genitals, and consequently also my feet, at exactly the same level as hers too. We lay like that quite a long time, in silence. We were both breathing heavily, perhaps because she was feeling hot, and I, because I didn't know how to do something which had not happened for such a long time - a year, I think, or perhaps two. I made a small hole through the canes and put my hand through it. I immediately touched her warm body. I fumbled blindly, as if I were putting my hand in a bag to draw a lottery ticket, and landed on the elastic of her knickers, which I pulled down. She raised her body in an arc to help me take them off. As I was lying with my head resting against the fence and looking in quite a different direction, I did not see her do this, but I was able to follow the movement exactly because, for one thing, one's hands communicate a sense of volume and weight and consequently sometimes see more than one's eyes. The images you get through your hands are always three-dimensional. You look at pictures with your eyes and at a sculpture with your hands; that is why you always want to touch a piece of sculpture. Not because you want to feel the material, as some people think, but simply because you want to see it better.

I didn't say anything else. I touched her with my hands several times more, and eventually turned her whole body sideways, crushing it against the canes. I took my clothes off too. I was holding her against the fence with one hand when the shade reached her body, giving me an unpleasant sensation of cold. I withdrew my hand and dressed again, as did she.

She started talking next day. We were again separated by the fence between the two enclosures. She said she had something important to tell me, something very important indeed, and she was glad the fence was between us, because it gave her a great sense of tranquility. She began by saying there were days on which places or even persons you didn't know of hadn't seen or heard of for years kept cropping up, and you suddenly started hearing all sorts of things about them all at once. In the course of a few hours, for instance, you would discover that a childhood friend you had lost sight of for ages was living in New York, had married a Negress, and had written a book about birds that was coming out soon. You would pick up the first bit of information from the newspaper for instance, the second would be casually mentioned by a friend or acquaintance, and you would hear the third in the bus or the tram. Then till the day of your death you would never again hear a single thing about the person or the place you had found out such a lot of things about in the course of a single day.

I listened in amusement. Actually I agreed completely with what she said. I waited for her to go on, but suddenly she said she had forgotten why she had made that long speech. She couldn't even remember what she had been leading up to.

'You had something important to tell me,' I said.

She kept me waiting for five minutes while she pondered about this highly important matter. Then she repeated that now she couldn't remember it.

'Then it must have been pretty unimportant.'

'On the contrary,' she said. 'What did I say when I arrived?'

'That you had something very important to tell me.'

'What were the exact words I used?'

'I can't remember the exact words, but that's what they amounted to. You seemed rather worried.'

We went on wrangling for half, and hour and then she went off.

We met again inside the house, but hardly exchanged a gesture, let alone a word. I realized that it was impossible for us to talk without that fence between us.

When she turned up next day I asked her straight out whether she remembered what she had been going to tell me. Yes, she said, but she no longer felt like talking about it. Yesterday she had felt like it, but

53

today she didn't. Perhaps it wasn't worth the trouble. I asked her if it was anything serious.

'Pretty serious,' she said.

'Was it about me,' I asked.

'No.'

'Was it about the two of us?'

'Perhaps it was. And anyway, whatever we say is always about the two of us, even if we try talking about something else.'

* * * * *

I was walking in the desert. My feet sank in the scorching sand. Fortunately there was a dune that broke the vast expanse of sand for a long stretch, so I could walk in the shade. I was not alone. The others walked in the shade too. There were three or four of them. Sometimes I thought there were three and sometimes four. The archeologist, a thin English man with a red, hairy face, was certainly one of them. We were looking for desert roses. Desert roses, for the benefit of the uninformed, are made from petrified sand. Towards evening we stopped and sat down, and just when we were going to lie down and go to sleep I felt something hard under my back. I searched in the sand with my hands and discovered a thin, flat rock. But it wasn't a rock. It was a piece of square, black marble, in which I saw the reflection of my face when I lit a match. We all started vigorously digging away in the sand, and that was how we spent the night. At dawn a black and white checkered marble floor appeared. We walked about on it, marvelling, and noticed that it was warm on the white squares and cool on the black ones, as if both warmth and coolness came from below, i.e. from the marble. We wondered what the floor had been used for and who had built it. Arabs? Ancient Egyptians? Or visitors from another planet? But suddenly the wind rose and moved the sand and covered the floor again. In the sun-laden wind I heard a voice. It was my wife's. 'We've got to find a way out,' she repeated several times, and suddenly the desert shrank, turned into Luisa's face, and the checker pattern reappeared on her blouse. We were lying on either side of the cane fence that separated us, looking at each other through the gaps.

'We've got to find a way out,' she repeated.

'I don't believe in looking for solutions,' I replied. 'They come of their own accord.'

'I don't agree.'

'What do you mean?'

'I think solutions have got to be looked for.'

'It's no good discussing solutions until you've told me what the problem is.'

'We haven't got a solution to anything.'

'It's no good talking at random. Take us two, for instance.'

'Certainly, let's take us two.'

'Let us consider what solutions there might be to the problem of us two.'

'I might consider suicide,' she said.

'Are you serious?'

'No, I'm merely suggesting a possible solution.'

'Is that what you wanted to tell me yesterday?'

'No, that was something more complicated.'

'In what way more complicated?'

'In what it leads to.'

'Perhaps it's a matter for action rather than discussion. Perhaps the solution will gradually emerge quite naturally and of its own accord.'

'Let's discuss it.'

'Perhaps that would be best. But not now. Tomorrow.'

That night wind battered the cane labyrinth, and rain did the rest. The havoc was irreparable. Next morning I piled all the canes in the middle of the field and set fire to them. I watched the pyre blazing with the patience of an Indian. My wife was at the window.

After the destruction of the labyrinth her refusal to talk was mere pique. I badly wanted to get rid of the bogy that had established itself between us, the mysterious shadow I filled with the images and ideas that passed through my mind. I had to think of some way of getting her to overcome her reticence, though I didn't really know if it was reticence. I started making a lot of letters, including all the letters of the alphabet. I made about sixty altogether, because I wanted different vowels of the same type, and of course at least two examples of every consonant. When I had finished I took them down to the riverbed. I fixed around twenty little wooden board in the ground, gave Luisa some drawing pins, and told her to stick any letters she chose to the boards or, if she felt like it, make up a complete sentence with them. Then I took up a position about a hundred yards away. It seemed to be merely my usual way of checking from a distance the legibility and clarity of some lettering, but in reality it was a stratagem to get my wife to indicate some thought or idea about herself or the two of us. I sat down about a hundred yards away, and then lay down. In front of me I saw the twenty dark little boards standing out against the white of the riverbed that went all the way down to the sea. The first letter to appear was an I, followed by a blank, then came an H, which somehow created the impression of a gallows. This was followed by the letters A, V and E. Like a child learning to read, I repeated to myself the phrase 'I have'. Then came the letters D, E and C, and I guessed correctly that the next word was going to be 'decided'. But what had she decided? The words I HAVE DECIDED TO appeared, followed by an M, an S, another S, a T, a V, an X and finally a Z. I HAVE DECIDED TO MSSYVXZ. Why hadn't she had the courage to finish the sentence? I got up and went over to her and asked her in a really loud voice what she had decided. Tell me, I said. She dropped the letters and walked back towards the house.

After that she spent her time reading. I never wondered what it was that she read with such passion.

57

Or perhaps she wasn't reading at all. Perhaps she just sat there all day with an open book in front of her while her mind was elsewhere. Perhaps she was thinking all the time about whatever it was that was on her mind, or perhaps she was gazing into space without thinking anything at all. Of course, spending hours staring at the page of a book crowded with little black squiggles is a thing that happens to everyone at times; it's like having a swarm of ants on one's hands. I kept an eye on her as I busied myself round the house with my paint pots. When I got to where she was I painted a line about half an inch thick from floor to ceiling. I ended by painting a line like that in every room in the house, because Luisa changed rooms every two or three hours. There was a room with a blue line, and another with a green one, and in the end there were eighteen lines altogether, each in a different color, thus allowing each room to be known by name, e.g. the orange room, the red room, etc. etc. And doing all this gave me an excuse to be near her, offering her a chance to confide in me and unburden herself. But I often grew impatient and asked her what it was that she had decided. One fine day she grew irritable. She said that she had started making up the first sentence that came into her head, and it had ended with an incomprehensible word because she did not know the ending herself.

Then she walked off.

I did not follow her. I was busy with the lavatory door. My idea was to paint on it the symbol I had devised in Rome for the International Centre for the Abolition of Language Barriers - an organization concerned with Africa, I think. It was one of those symbols intended to indicate to the illiterate things of primary importance, such as railway, post office, lavatory, etc. etc. I had been asked to design a symbol for lavatory. My design showed a man sitting on a cube. A black man on a white cube. I put a white disc in the man's belly and a black disc in the white cube. I considered this highly appropriate, because it indicated that there was something in the belly that should be transferred to the cube. That symbol is certainly to be found in Africa today. A symbol in a continent in ferment. The more symbols arrive in Africa, the more white men are killed or leave.

And now I had painted it on the door of the lavatory in the country house.

That afternoon, while I was leaning against the outside of the house, looking at the crazy paving that formed a kind of irregular footpath all round it, the superstition mechanism suddenly started up. If I managed to walk all round the house without stepping on any of the lines, I said to myself, Luisa would come clean. I must walk normally not shortening my stride if I were to step on one of the innumerable lines. I accepted this challenge. After a quick glance to see how to dole out my footsteps, I started walking along the wall, making sure that my shoes landed properly on the stones, and I reached the corner without once hesitating or going wrong. But when I stopped I had the feeling that the test hadn't proved anything. I don't know why. Perhaps it had been too easy. Perhaps I had cheated. At any rate, that is what I felt. Though I had tried to walk at a natural, easy, constant pace, I could not swear that I had not imperceptibly checked and controlled every step. But for the fact that I had slightly shortened my stride to gain a few inches at the fourth or fifth stone, I should certainly have landed on a line. However, I had no doubt that I should have felt dissatisfied whatever I had done. Because as soon as I enter the web of superstition I set a dreadful mechanism in motion. I begin devising one task after the other. An almost agonizing crescendo of difficult tasks. Each more difficult that the last.

Something of the sort happened to me in Rome when I took part in the Alitalia competition. Incidentally, I am not really superstitious at all. I am a complete sceptic in the matter. Black cats, the number thirteen, all that sort of thing leave me completely cold. But whenever I am faced with a really severe test or a really knotty problem superstition gets the better of me. I don't know if it can really be called superstition. The fact remains that when I am in such a situation I set myself difficult or impossible tasks. If you manage to do this or that, I say to myself, afterwards everything will be alright. That time in Rome was the task to touch the legs of a woman who was sitting with her husband on a divan in the big booking hall at the airport. Oh no, that was another time. Not that the details matter. Perhaps I felt I had to touch the woman's legs to assure myself of a trouble-free flight to New York; very probably that was the reason, in fact, because I am a bad air passenger. In any case, I sat down next to the couple and dropped something at the woman's feet. I bent down, and was just about to accidentally touch her leg while carrying out the innocent and natural movement of picking it up when the part of me that had taken charge and imposed the task suddenly insisted that I must touch her thigh in the classic area that extends from the top of the stocking to the knickers. That's just an example to show how a relatively easy test can turn into an exceedingly difficult one. I protested at the imposition. It's not fair, I said to myself, it's not fair. Meanwhile the two got up and walked away, and I had no alternative but to follow them. They went to the bar and sat down by the big window that looks out on to the runways. I sat down at the next table, ordered something, and devised a complicated scheme, the first part of which consisted, I think, in causing my wedding ring to roll under the table at which the two were sitting. But the waiter got there first and picked it up. So I started shouting at him, pretended to stumble, and managed to end up under the tablecloth in front of which the couple were sitting. In a flash I took my bearings, identified the woman's legs and the area of thigh between the stockings and the knickers, shot out an arm like a snake darting at something, touched it, quickly withdrew it, and emerged from under the tablecloth. The woman merely let out a slight squeak, and her husband asked her what was the matter, while I hid my head between my hands as if I had hurt it. Then I went off, and all was well. Half and hour later I was airborne and on the way to America.

Since then I had not relapsed into the pitfalls of superstition. It is just as well that there should be these long period of peace, otherwise one would go mad.

Such were the thoughts that passed through my mind as I went back into the house and began wandering from room to room. I stopped in front of an open window and leant out to look at something, and at that moment the mechanism started up again. Just as I had expected. When superstition has once got hold of you, it isn't as though you could draw back at any moment. The order I gave myself was to make my way along the brick cornice, barely two inches wide, that went round under the windows somewhere between ten and fifteen feet above ground level, encircling the house as a belt encircles a pair of trousers. I climbed out of the window, put my toes on the cornice, and started making my way along the wall, holding on to nails or stones protruding from the peeling whitewash. Also the gutters were of some help. The going was very difficult, but all went well until I found myself stranded half-way along, because after that there was nothing to hold on to and it was impossible to go on. I stayed there for a long time, with my face to the wall, my toes on the cornice, my left hand holding a nail and my right a crack in the whitewash. I knew that if I succeeded in this task Luisa would come out with everything that was on her mind. So I went on with my precarious balancing act - until I started trembling as if with a nervous spasm. Perhaps my muscles were going to sleep, I did not know whether to go on or to go back. Fortunately someone propped a ladder against the wall and I managed to get hold of it. I came down.

My wife was waiting for me at the bottom. 'Why on earth did you do it?' she exclaimed. 'Tell me, why?' She too was in the grip of anxiety about something she could not understand. 'I'll never tell you, never,' I replied maliciously.

* * * * *

Arrows and circles are very important, in my opinion. I mean arrows and circles as symbols. They are very important indeed. Arrows send you to places, make you lift weights or go down on your knees. Circles stop you, imprison your eyes, make things like Coca-Cola or whatever else it may be, even though you are wanting to look at something else. The circle and the arrow, in short, are as important as the words 'free' and 'new' which, at any rate according to Ogilvy, have the greatest drawing power in advertising. Besides, arrows make an impact inside you, because everyone's eye follows a white arrow on a blue field or a yellow arrow on a black one, even when they are not there. Perhaps the ultimate arbiter of everything, sending us here or there and making us do all the things that we do now, is an arrow.

Thus, after the complete breach with my wife, I started painting arrows. Since arriving at the house I had hardly seen a human soul. True, I had seen one or two carters in the distance, and had spoken to the lorry driver that day when I wanted to check my Ts, Ls and Ps at speed, but since then I had seen nobody. But I knew that there were people in the area, beyond the canes and the trees. So I put up a number of arrows about forty paces apart. They started at point x, passed the front of the house, and then went off in the direction of the cane-brake. The result was that I got to know everyone who lived in or frequented these parts: peasants, men who came to shoot, an old swineherd, two soldiers from a camp farther down the river - they were on summer manoeuvres - their officer, who was a captain, and some boys. (The captain was looking for a spent cartridge case.) None of them knew why they came this way, but I did. They were under the spell of the arrows, and simply followed them. I just lay near the well and watched.

The accident took me completely by surprise. I heard a cry behind the house, and hurried to see what had happened. I dashed through the cane brake, and farther on, when I reached the line of little hillocks that fell steeply into the riverbed, I spotted her almost at once. I hurried down to the riverbed and picked her up. Her face was dirty and blood-stained, and she might have been dead. But she opened her eyes and pushed me away with her hands. I went away. She got up by herself and washed away the blood in the trickle of water in the middle of the riverbed, abusing me all the time. She said I had tried to kill her, forcing her to fling herself down from the height. No, not directly, but by means of my arrows. In fact I had placed the last arrow at the edge, and of course it was an inducement to go on. Why had I done it? I tried explaining that I had merely wanted to round off the series, I had needed a logical conclusion, it was simply a question of rhythm, an open point at the top and a closed point at the bottom. However, I was inclined to agree that the last arrow was capable of being interpreted as a vague invitation to suicide. But Luisa refused to listen to me. She left Milan the same evening. Later I learnt that she had broken two ribs in her fall, but at the time it seemed as if little or nothing had happened.

Why are things that get lost,
for instance,
so unwilling to be found?

The ashes filled the whole area of the camp from beyond the red villa which was the headquarters of the building to the single hut that housed us. They were the ashes of huts which a month before had been swept up by typhoid fever that sent about a thousand prisoners to the next world. The occupants of our hut were the only survivors. Our feet were in those ashes all day long, and so were our eyes. Mixed up in the ashes were long nails, bolts, bits of charred wood, all the stuff that could be used for making barricades round our mattresses as a protection against the bullets that whizzed past our ears every evening. One man found a bit of metal sheeting with which he made himself a kind of helmet, and others put old cans over their heads. But all those things were only palliatives, because death kept dodging us. The commandant would come in at all hours of the night, whenever he felt like it, and the next morning we had to carry out the dead and bury them under the ashes. Then we had to stand in line, whereupon the invariable routine followed. The prisoner who had stolen the commandant's watch was ordered to step forward and, as no one stepped forward, the punishment continued. In the first few days nearly a dozen of us were killed, including the sick man; he was hit three times, as if the commandant had kept on aiming in the same direction. At first we though the man had died of his illness, but when we stripped him to steal his clothes before burying him we discovered he had been shot. There were three holes in his body. Three holes, each with a black, charred edge. It was obvious he had no blood left in him.

That was the day when we grew desperate and rounded on the Polish priest. It was up to him to find a way of getting us out of this hell, we told him, because he believed in God, and we didn't, and if he died he would go to heaven, and we shouldn't. We called him a liar and a humbug. We tore to shreds the little black bible he had in his pocket. We wanted no more prayers, or sermons, we said. What we wanted was action, and he had better do something and do something quickly. For three or four days we boycotted him completely; we kept as far away from him as possible, and when he approached one group or another for the sake of a little human company it immediately broke up; everyone shunned him as if her were a leper. Several times we saw him kneeling in the ashes and praying with his head in his hands.

So it went on until one evening, just when the commandant was about to hand out the cabbage leaves, he stepped forward and went down on his knees in front of him. He said it was he who had stolen the watch. The commandant took out his revolver, pointed it at the back of his neck, and asked him where the watch was. He said he had thrown it away in the ashes. The officer filled the air with a freezing laugh. He made him rise to his feet again. He said he didn't like martyrs, and he certainly wasn't the thief. He ordered him back to the ranks and began handing out the cabbage leaves.

I know that a man can turn into a cat. Particularly if he sets his mind to it. Not that he grows fur or a tail, but somehow he turns into a cat. I had special reasons of my own for wanting to turn into a cat. In particular, I wanted cat's eyes, because cats can see in the dark, and that interested me. Not so much to be able to see the commandant and the direction in which his revolver was pointing. No, that wasn't it at all. My reason was quite a different one. I was falling in love with the pretty Czech girl who slept with her husband in the bunk underneath mine. I didn't know her name, and never did. I don't know if she realized what was happening. She may have done, because we exchanged glances every now and then while walking about in the ashes looking for things, but that was all. We also exchanged glances while munching our cabbage leaves like rabbits. She was a better rabbit than I, she munched more delicately and quite noiselessly, and that made me aware of her femininity and excited me. At night everyone else slept heavily, but her breath was quiet and warm, and seemed to warm my bunk. Then she and her husband started making love. They did it every night and I lay in my bunk with my head dangling over the side better to hear them. But I also wanted to be able to see them, and that was why I wanted to turn into a cat. I kept peering into the darkness, and on the second night I thought I was beginning to be able to make out something, but wasn't sure. All the details of the inside of the hut were so firmly implanted in my mind that I might have been seeing things only because my mind projected onto them in the dark. However that may be, gradually I managed to make out the bunk in which the Russians slept, and then the elephant man's corner, and then the floor. In the end I could see everything. I may have been helped by some holes in the ceiling made by the commandant's bullets. That may have been the source of the faint light reflected in the interior of the hut.

At all events in the end I was able to see them making love. His back and her excited face and white, splayed legs. We began looking at each other while she made love and I lay there with my head dangling over the side.

On the fourth or fifth night I let my arm dangle too, and she, in the midst of her love-making, took my hand and squeezed it. This went on for several nights. She made love, looked at me, and we held hands. Her husband held her with his other hand, and perhaps that was why he never noticed it.

Whenever I tie up a parcel,
for instance,
I end by finding myself tied up inside it.

Fortunately the mole episode cropped up. Otherwise life would have gone on the same way. It was as if I were drunk. Luisa's departure had left me stranded in a kind of empty tunnel, and I could not concentrate on anything. Vague thoughts drifted through my mind like balloons in the wind. Also I slept a great deal. And I think I barricaded myself in the house for several days, passing the time by holding my hands to cracks to shut out the light.

I discovered the moles when I started wandering about outside the house again. The first thing I noticed was that my foot sank at a spot where the earth was soft and powdery. I looked down, and saw that the whole area was criss-crossed by long, wavy lines of swollen earth. I realized at once that moles must be responsible, and I decided to use the peasant method of frightening them away, that is, by tying stones to pieces of tin and letting the wind do the rest. I knocked sticks into the ground and connected them with wire, from which I hung stones and pieces of tin. By the time I had finished the job it was dark. I went into the house, had something to eat, and waited for the wind to get up, as it did every evening, though it varied in strength. It came down the river valley and blew itself over the sea. Sure enough, at about nine o'clock the pieces of tin started beating against the stones. I flung myself on the bed and listened through the open window. The noise struck me as rather feeble, so I got up and released all the shutters in the house that held them against the wall for heaven knows how long, and they duly started creaking and banging. The empty rooms reverberated with the din. I can't explain it, but the whole thing gradually acquired musical meaning, as if the house had turned into a big musical instrument. I listened, and made out the tin sheet motif interwoven with the banging shutters. That night i went to sleep late, very late indeed.

I can't remember now whether I was coming from the mill or going towards it, but at all events I was in the middle of the river, as usual bending down to look at something or other. Then I found myself standing erect again and looking all round, and when that happens you can't be sure whether you are going somewhere or coming from it. I walked off with lowered head, as if my intention were to sink. One step after another on the stones. Often I crouched down until I was almost on the ground, looking at the little runways along which small black creatures with feelers made their way. I must have killed about forty of them with an old nail I had in my pocket. Then I used it to clean my fingernails, and threw it away. My head was turning and my body felt light and unsteady, so I filled my pockets with stones to give myself weight and substance. Then I took them out one by one, moistened them with my tongue, and dropped them in the riverbed, assuring myself that I should be able to find them all again later. I walked on like this for about a hundred yards, or until I had no more stones left, and then turned in my tracks and started picking them up again, identifying them by the small patch of moisture I had left on each with my tongue. I managed to find about thirty this way, but no more because by this time the saliva had dried up. However, my attention was distracted by a box of Swedish matches. Before opening it I put it to my ear and shook it, to see whether it was empty. It was not, but it contained three used matches only. Someone had lit three cigarettes, or three cigars, or whatever else it might have been. But why had he put them back in the box instead of throwing them away? So from the matchbox my mind passed to consideration of its owner. He had left something of himself behind, evidence of an idiosyncrasy or some instinctive meanness. I was filled with great curiosity. At eight o'clock that evening I was in the tobacconist's near the bridge. An old woman, a bench, a sack of salt, about twenty packets of cigarettes of various kinds, candles, and a box of cheap cigars. The old woman told me she sold wax matches, and kitchen matches, but not Swedish matches. Perhaps the other tobacconist stocked them, the one on the main road, in fact she was sure he did. So I went to see him. He was a small, nervy man, aged about fifty.

77

Yes, he said, he sold Swedish matches.

'To whom?'

'To anyone who asks for them, of course.'

'To whom have you sold them recently?'

'But why do you want to know?'

'Because I'm interested.'

'Are you from the police?'

'Yes.'

'Well, then, the artillery captain buys them, the one sleeping in the tent down by the river, and so does the owner of the filling station, and the man they call Titobu. And anyone else who asks for them.'

'What matches do you use yourself?'

'Wax matches and kitchen matches. Sometimes I also use Swedish matches.'

'What are you using now?'

'What do you mean?'

'What matches have you got in your pocket?'

'I don' know.'

'Have a look and see.'

'But I don't wish to.'

'Then put your hands up, and I'll see. Come on, up with your hands.'

He ended up by putting his hands up, and I went through his pockets. I laid the contents on the bench. I am passionately interested in the things people have in their pockets. A piece of string appeared, three corks, a small role of wire, some small change and two boxes of matches, one wax and one Swedish.

'Why do you have two boxes?'

'Well you know how it is...'

'And where's your handkerchief?'

'I haven't got one.'

'What! No handkerchief?'

'I hardly ever blow my nose.'

'But what do you use when you do blow your nose?'

'A handkerchief.'

'But what do you do if you haven't got one?'

'I go and fetch one.'

'Why don't you admit that sometimes you use your fingers?'

'No, I do not.'

'Show me your hands.'

He showed me his hands. They were filthy. I walked out without another word. I went back to the riverbed and looked for the artillery captain. I met two other people first. I'm not sure, but I think I also met a girl. Yes, I also met a girl. The captain was in his tent. There was a tank about twenty yards away.

'Excuse me, captain, but may I ask you a question?' He was half asleep and was writing a letter. 'Do you use Swedish matches?'

'Yes. Why?'

'I found this box in the river. Is it yours?'

'It may be. Why?'

'Pardon my curiosity, but why did you put three used matches back in the box?'

I showed him the three matches with black, charred heads.

'In the first place I don't know that it is mine, and in the second place I don't see the object of the question.'

'It interests me.'

'What does?'

'Finding out why someone puts used matches back in the box. There must be a reason for it, and I'm determined to find out.'

'And then what?'

'I shall stop thinking about it. Otherwise I shall be haunted by the problem.'

The captain got up, walked out of the tent, and started talking to the crew of ten tank. I stayed and watched them for a time, and then went off.

Next day I went to see the man at the filling station. His pump was on the left bank, beside the bridge. It was an old-fashioned pump, the kind you don't see any longer, that looks like a man standing up. But next to it was a very modern office made of glass and steel, very light and transparent, looking very incongruous in that part of the world, and attractive perhaps for that reason. I sat on the parapet of the bridge and had a good look at the man. He wore a blue boiler-suit that fitted him snugly at the waist, and he was sitting in the space between the pump and the office, where there was a pile of oil tins. After a time he put a cigar in his mouth, but he didn't feel comfortable, got up, rearranged his seat, and then sat down again. He looked at me. I pretended to be looking at a dog that was walking along the street. The dog stopped and looked first at me and then at him. Then it moved away into the shadow of the other parapet of the bridge and lay down in the dust. The petrol pump man picked up a stone and threw it, gently, not to frighten the dog, but obviously to gain its confidence. The stone described a parabola before landing at its feet, and it sniffed it. The petrol pump man then started talking to it, but I had the feeling that his questions were really directed to me. Who was I? Where did I come from? Where was I going? So I didn't answer. I was a chicken thief, was I?

The dog rose to its feet, walked off across the bridge, and disappeared round the corner. Not till then did the man take out a box of Swedish matches to light his cigar. He selected a match and rubbed it on the box. He lit his cigar, quickly extinguished the match, and put it back in the box. I got up and strolled across to him.

'Pardon my curiosity, but may I ask you something? Why do you put used matches back in the box?'

He pointed to the petrol pump. 'As a safety precaution,' he said. 'The whole place could blow up.'

'But if you have extinguished the match, why bother?'

'Better safe than sorry.'

I showed him the box of Swedish matches I had in my pocket.

'Was this box yours?'

The petrol pump man examined it, opened it, and looked at one of the used matches.

'No,' he said positively.

'How can you tell?'

'That match was used by a cigarette smoker. You can tell by the amount of charred wood. Look at one of mine.'

He showed me one of his. It was black nearly all the way down.

'Don't you see?' he said. 'To light a cigar you need nearly a whole match, the wood had to burn too. Actually I often burn my fingers.'

He handed me back the box of matches. I tossed it in the palm of my hand before putting it back in my pocket. Then I took my bearings and went away.

I went back to the river to look for the person who had thrown away the matchbox containing three spent matches. I have to get to the bottom of things, otherwise they form a solid knot inside my head, and I can feel it confusing me, and also weighing down on all the other things I have accumulated inside my head in the course of forty years. This was the first time I had felt that kind of knot. I tried tackling other problems to distract myself, in the hope of being able to think about other things, and I thought I was getting over it, but I was wrong. So I started stopping people again and asking them what kind of matches they used, and so on, and so forth, and that was how it came about that I eventually reached the sea, where they told me that the character known as Titobu was to be found. And in fact there he was, just as they had said, sitting on the shore, with his hat resting over a melancholy pair of eyes.

I sat down beside him and gazed at the sea too. Eventually he started talking. Talking about the sea, which he referred to as That Strange Individual. Had I had any dealings with That Strange Individual? he asked me, pointing at it. No, I said, I had not. That Strange Individual ruined me, he said, and launched into a long story about some land he had bought and the money he had spent on it. But then That Strange Individual had swallowed it all up. It had been gradually eroded by a hitherto non-existent current that might have sprung up when they extended the harbor at Ancona. It had worn away his land bit by bit, presenting him in return with dead dogs, pieces of cork and other objects that That Individual had been unable to keep down. It had even presented him with a dead man, and then with a whale that was said to have been killed by nuclear radiation and no one had been willing to touch. He had managed to tow it out to sea in a boat, but the current swept it back and dumped it on his land again. This had happened four or five times, and eventually he had got tired of it and buried it. Of course he had hoped that the erosion would cease, because he wanted to sell off the remainder of his land in lots, but no such luck. That Individual had swallowed it all, including the boundary marks. Now he spent the whole day waiting to see whether That Individual would make up his mind to withdraw and give him back his land. He had not given up hope. Perhaps the moon might come to his aid; in fact at low tide some of it reappeared. There were a few yards of beach every morning, but then it vanished again.

I asked him for a light, and he handed me a box of Swedish matches. I put a cigarette in my mouth and opened the box. There were some used matches among the unused ones. I lit my cigarette and handed him back the box. I dropped the match on the ground between us. I noticed that he did not put the box straight back in his pocket. I offered him a cigarette, but he said he didn't smoke. In that case why did he buy matches? I asked. As if it were the most natural thing in the world, he picked up the match I had dropped and started sharpening it with his pen-knife. Then he closed the knife and put the spent match back in the box.

'Do you collect matches?' I asked him pointblank.

'Yes,' he said. He opened the box and showed me its contents.

He picked out a spent match the end of which he had sharpened for some inexplicable reason.

'I use them as toothpicks,' he explained.

I had not thought of that. I looked at the three matches in my box. The unburnt part had not been sharpened so they could not have belonged to Titobu.

I walked back along the middle of the riverbed. My head was turning, because of the light, which at certain times of day made all the trees on the banks dance, as well as the stones all round me. I found a bank of sand on which there was some straggling vegetation, some thistles, and a big mallow with broad, hairy leaves. I knelt down with my face to the sand to look horizontally at the stalks and the few tremulous shadows on the sand. Then I rose to my feet again, took off my tennis shoes, and walked on the sand until I reached a big hole. The mud at the bottom, cracked by the sun, looked like a metropolis seen from above. I went down into the hole, lifted the slabs of dried mud, and felt in the cracks for any moisture that might be left underneath. Then I climbed out again and looked in the direction of the sea.

In the mirror of water beyond the cane-brakes, the mud flats, and the marshes of the estuary I could clearly make out an old Austrian submarine half buried in the sand. A boat detached itself from the submarine, made towards the cane-brakes, and disembarked five sailors wearing old-fashioned white uniforms, boots and puttees. They advanced cautiously in single file. They passed quite close to me and I saw their red faces, red hair and eyes clear as water. The last of them was carrying a greenish box, which every now and then he

85

cautiously rested on the stones. I followed them for about two miles, keeping a short distance behind them, until they reached the railway bridge that crosses the river just where the mountains begin. Cautiously and tensely they went to one of the arches of the bridge. Then they made their way to a sandy hollow, where they sat down. I peeped out furtively and watched them. They were helping themselves to black bread out of an aluminium container. The bread was hard, and they dipped it in water before eating it. The whistle of an approaching train galvanized them into action. One of them went to the edge of the hollow to look at the bridge while the others stood round the mysterious box and raised a kind of plunger. The train emerged from behind the last hill and reached the bridge. The Austrian sailor at the edge of the hollow signalled with his hand. A tremendous crack rent the sky as if were made of glass, and there was a shower of dust, bits of wood and brickwork, and metal fragments. The five Austrians made off towards the estuary and disappeared, and I stayed looking at the catastrophe they had caused. The air was full of piercing cries. I moved. In the smoke I met Italian soldiers, bleeding and their uniforms in tatters. Others lay dead on the ground. Someone came running up, he was a carter, and we began lifting wounded and dying men onto his cart. I came to a villa, and knocked the brass ring knocker on the massive door. I turned, but the horse and cart and wounded had disappeared. I was alone and did not know how I had got there.

A still attractive woman of about forty opened the door.

'Yes?' she said.

'Forgive my curiosity, but may I ask you a question? How many times has the bridge over the river been destroyed?'

'Twice, as far as I know,' she said. 'It was carried away by floods in 1924, and in 1944 it was blown up by partisans.'

'And in the First World War?'

'Not as far as I know, but I've no idea. But my mother would know.'

'I should be most obliged if you would ask her?'

'But why do you want to know, if I may ask?'

'I'm writing a history of the river.'

We went upstairs into the sitting-room. She introduced me to her mother, a shivering old woman.

'Yes,' she said. 'The Austrians blew it up in 1916.'

'What happened?'

'They landed sailors with an explosive charge from a submarine.'

'Were there any casualties?'

'Yes there were a great many killed and wounded. Some were brought here.'

'Who brought them?'

'I think it was a young man with a horse and cart.'

'That was me.'

'But how can that be possible? How old are you?'

'Forty-five.'

'But you weren't born then.'

'That has nothing to do with it.'

I lit myself a cigarette and looked round for an ashtray. But I couldn't see one, and stood there holding the spent wax match in mid-air.

'Give it to me,' the younger woman said, and made as if to take the match from me and put it down somewhere. I didn't let her, but put it back in the box. This natural and automatic action made me think of the three used matches again, and a possible answer to the problem flashed through my mind. It struck me that the owner of the box might well be a frequent visitor to this villa.

'Do you know the artillery captain?' I asked the younger woman with a malicious smile. She flushed with embarrassment and sat down beside her aged mother.

I realized at once that the shaft had gone home. And perhaps I had solved my problem. Perhaps the captain was her lover. At all events, having found a possible answer to the problem, I lost interest in comparing my assumptions with reality. I looked at the two women, smiled, and my mind moved elsewhere. I got up and began walking round the room. Then so many ideas exploded in my head, crowding on each other's heels, and I started saying a lot of disconnected words, verbs in particular. It was as if my stomach were full of words and I had to bring them up.

I went back to the riverbed. Black patches of shadow were scattered along the banks. I noticed three isolated stones in a hole in the sand. Actually there were four or five or even more, but I didn't count them, all I cared about was gathering them together, piling them into a little heap. When I had finished I started looking for all the other holes in which stones were scattered, to gather them together before night fell, or before autumn came in a month's time and began filling the riverbed with water and covering them and forming whirlpools.

By the time I got back to the house it was nine o'clock, and I lit candles. I wanted to go to bed. But my mind was not at rest. I gathered all the chairs, and all my papers, brushes, suitcases and strips of cardboard, into the middle of the room. Thus the things of the world were uniting, at any rate those by which I was surrounded. I flung myself exhausted on the bed, but then got up and lit a candle again. I realized I was the only isolated thing, the only one not united to anything. I dashed out of the house and down to the river not knowing where I was going. I knew only that I had to take hold of something or somebody. But there was darkness round me, and silence. I began running, probably towards the sea, because the wind was behind me, and I knew that at night the wind came from the mountains. But I was not sure. It might also be blowing up the river-bed, up and up, who knows where. I wanted to run into something, a tree, for instance, and at least seize hold of that. So I decided to make for one bank or the other. But it was night, and my eyes beneath my perspiring brow saw only that it was night.

When I drop things,
for instance,
it's not my fault, but theirs.

The days passed in spite of the nightly three bullets that often landed in someone's flesh. It was like a chronic illness. We no longer waited for the commandant with any particular trepidation, but the shots startled us out of our sleep. Those who were hit of course woke up at once. There were some groans and whines, and that was all. We buried them under the ashes the next morning. The fearful thing now was hunger. We began trying to catch crows.

Our first idea had been to try and catch the rats we heard scuttling about on the ashes at night, but we never discovered where they went during the day. They must have had deep and undiscoverable holes under the headquarters villa. But the crows were always there, either perched on the barbed wire or taking off and settling on the branches of the trees outside. They seemed to cling to the air or the clouds rather than to fly, and when they landed on the ground they looked as awkward and walked as unsteadily as a man who has fallen from a ladder. At least three or four times a day I nearly managed to grab one, but at the last moment it always flew away. One day the elephant man actually ended up with a handful of feathers in his hand; he had caught one by the tail.

Then one day the earth started trembling again, and so did the hut and the barbed wire and the branches of the trees. The front was approaching, and the fear of death returned. There is nothing worse than dying when rescue is near. That morning the S.S. officer again ordered the person who had stolen his watch to step forward, and again nobody did. Of course the thief may already have been dead, but in any case no one, not even the commandant himself, expected anyone to step forward. Meanwhile the crows flew overhead, not daring to land anywhere. All that trembling obviously terrified them, and they flew backwards and forwards as if they had gone mad. Eventually, at about four in the afternoon, they started dropping to the ground like stones. They dropped everywhere, on the hut roof and in the ashes. Most of them were still alive, but exhausted; they spread their wings on the ground and limped. The commandant emerged from his villa, revolver in hand, and started picking them off one by one.

That day the Czech decided to kill the commandant. I don't know why no one had thought of it before. In any case, it was the only thing to do. He was nearly always drunk, so it would be easy. We decided that after killing him we would kill the guard dogs, using long hard bits of burnt wood as cudgels, and overpower the few guards, of whom there were about a dozen altogether. Someone produced a pickaxe - I don't know where he scrounged it from. We lay on our straw mattresses and waited.

An hour or two passed, or it may have been more, and then at last we heard his footsteps. They were irregular, as if he had only one leg, because you could hear the sound of one boot but not the other. Perhaps he was limping, or had lost a boot, or was leaning to one side and so had one of his legs out of balance completely. Also he was shouting incoherently. He may have been yelling orders into the air, or cursing the Americans who were advancing on the other side of the wood or were entrenched in that direction. The Czech was waiting for him behind the door with his pick in readiness, and his wife, lying in the bunk, turned her head and looked at me every so often. The German, who was obviously drunk, reached the outside of the hut and leant his hands against it. Then he began walking round it, striking it with his fists. At last he reached the door. You could hear him sobbing, sobbing as if her were holding his face in his hands. Then he quietened down. He had probably decided to come in. The Czech took a firmer grip of his pick, but the door did not open. This time three shots rang out from outside the hut - the German fired at the door and the walls beside it. The Czech slumped to the ground like a sack of potatoes. One of the three bullets had pierced the wood and struck him in the neck, and he died without a sound. His wife ran over to him and then came back and flung herself on the mattress in despair. One by one the others dropped off into a noisy sleep. I climbed down from my bunk and sat beside the girl. I laid my hand on her back to comfort her. Then I lay down beside her and stroked her hair. She went on weeping, resting her head on the rags that covered my chest. Her tears wetted my neck, and her trembling lips were open. Then she quietened down. She remained in my arms, and I told her that I loved her, and wanted to take her with me. I taught her four Italian words, the four stupid words that are always taught to foreigners, *amore, baci, buongiorno, buonasera*. Then she taught me four Czech words. Then we kissed and made love, and then we talked again. Neither of us understood very much of what the other said, but everything seemed clear, sweet, marvellous.

Next morning no one came to drive us out of the hut. I went back to my bunk and lay down again. She was in the bunk underneath. Her husband lay in a crumpled heap on the floor, embracing his death. The silence weighing down on the hut made a big impact; there was no barking of dogs, no shots, no crows. The world went on silently revolving. The daylight shone more and more brightly through the cracks. Everyone was thinking his own thoughts, but without communicating them to anyone else. Eventually the elephant man rose from his bunk and walked across the hut, dragging his feet. He was not going anywhere out of curiosity, but wanted to urinate. Slowly he opened the door, the hinges creaked, seeming to make a tremendous noise that nearly burst our eardrums. We stretched our necks to see what was happening outside. It was windy, bits of paper were flying about. There were footprints in the dried mud, and that was all. The elephant man went outside, and stopped in the midst of the silence and the flying bits of paper. Then the others went out, and so did I. We walked about on the muddy crust with the slowness of aged elephants. The rusty barbed wire fence seemed to be sticking into the air in a surrealist immobility, and the wind had blown more waste paper up against it. Then there were the grey ashes, and the open doors of the villa, and the untidiness of some things that had been dropped and abandoned outside the door and on the paving all round. Someone put his head in and then went inside. There was a knife stuck into a black loaf, breadcrumbs were scattered on the table, there were some broken glasses and a gum-boot. Then suddenly we saw two legs dangling. The German officer had hanged himself with a leather belt.

We all went to look, and we stayed there gazing at his grey face. Then, though not immediately, someone noticed the watch on his left wrist. It dawned on us that no one had stolen it. It was a cheap watch, worth very little, and it had stopped at a quarter past three. We went back into the open space among the scattered bits of paper, not yet believing that the war was over. But the gate was open, open on to an expanse of tall grass that the wind was blowing in our direction.

We gazed motionless at the open gate and the field and the grass beyond it. We gathered into a ball of flesh and rags in front of the gate. The woman, the woman I loved, put her arm in mine to show that I was her man, now and forever.

We remained there silently for an hour, or two, or three looking through the open gate, and no American or Russian or any other kind of liberating soldier appeared at the bottom of the field or our of the wood. Nothing happened at all. Suddenly I detached myself from the group and walked through the gate and out of the camp. I did it so quickly that I shook off the Czech girl's arm. Then I stopped, and lay down on the grass three or four yards outside the gate. There the air was different, it had a different smell, a different lightness. The others looked at me, and smiled, but did not follow. I rose to my feet and began walking in the direction of the wood. Then a voice called after me, and I stopped. My girl was running after me. We walked on together.

It was a butterfly that made me realize I was really free. I followed it in order to look at it. To look at its wings. Then I looked at the leaves of the trees, the branches, the clouds over the wood. The girl remained by my side. She tried to stop me, wanting me to look into her eyes, wanting to understand me. But how can a man who is re-embracing the world, looking at the woods and the clouds and the birds, concentrate on a petty domestic problem? Women are not interested in the world. All that matters to a woman is a man. In fact

I noticed several times that she sat down, encouraging me. She wanted to tell me some trivial and unimportant thing. But those stockings of hers that were white with chalk clashed with the landscape. I climbed a tree to get a better view of the surroundings. Not a town, or even a valley, was in sight. But there was a white, stony riverbed, and some American tanks were drawn up on the opposite bank. I climbed down and started hurrying along the tracks through the wood, with her behind me. Several times she seized my arm, not because she wanted to help me along, but probably because she felt she was losing me. Then she started weeping, and I slowed down. I told her various things, slapping the low branches of the trees as I did so. At a time like this, I said, when there was a whole world to rediscover and see again, love, a house, children, married life... I certainly did not finish this speech, and I could not understand what she said, for one thing because she spoke Czech. But I could very well imagine what she was trying to say. I caught her husband's name. She felt guilty. Neither of us could help feeling guilty, because both of us had wanted him to die. Now he had died, and for nothing.

At one point I turned round, and she was not there. But by now I could see the stone-lined riverbed beyond the sparse woodland, and on the opposite bank the long row of tanks with white stars on them. As I hurried along it struck me that they looked like a string of sausages. I took my clothes off to get rid of the lice.

Did I want to arrive clean? Perhaps I wanted to throw away the whole of my wretched life together with my clothes. Naked on the stones of the riverbed, and the sound of jazz over there. It was an Armstrong record, 'I Can't Give You Anything but Love, Baby.'

If we learnt to talk,
for instance,
animals would understand us better.

So I was found lying naked in a ditch, and unconscious and bleeding into the bargain. Can you imagine a country police sergeant trying to make head or tail of my story? In any case, it's difficult to talk to a fat man siting at your bedside in a small country hospital. I took his hand and asked him why his nails were dirty. This ruffled him, and he hid his hands in his uniform pocket. He began by telling me that I had been reported to the police by a woman named Maria Carpineti, of whom I had never heard. According to her story, I had entered her house, crept into her bed, and pretending to be her husband, tried to intertwine my legs with hers. Hence her frantic screams, and the swift intervention of various individuals, including her husband who ejected me from the house with kicks and blows. I remembered nothing of all this, though it was no doubt perfectly true because, after all, if you are found lying in a ditch naked, injured and unconscious, it's a sure sign that you've been up to something.

I tried explaining to the sergeant the real reason that might have led me surreptitiously to introduce myself into the woman's bed, namely the desire to feel united with someone. I had been in flight from total isolation, in a sense I had been fleeing from nature, that is, nature regarded as a sum-total of vegetation, stones, water and sky. I had also been fleeing because nature no longer really existed, only fragments were left, and they didn't count, it was just as if they didn't exist. Nature had changed completely, it had turned into what we ourselves manufactured: walls, posters, machinery and car interiors. That was the nature we lived in nowadays. It was a mistake to try and form a relationship with nature of the old type, made out of stones and rocks and the sky overhead. Perhaps it could be done, but one would have to start all over again from the beginning, learning, for instance, to sit on stones, stakes, and even on sharp points. But that would be a long story, taking us right back into prehistory. So that was why I needed to feel united with someone. Someone meant Man. Man meant humanity. So touching a woman's foot with my foot had meant touching the foot of mankind. Of course a husband who found someone in bed with his wife could hardly be expected to understand all this. To husbands, of course, it was simply a question of cuckoldry. This particular husband must have been the worst of the lot. Actually I thought I could remember him - a bow-legged man, the kind that takes his wife with his head on the commode and his eyes staring at grandpa's portrait. That was more or less the speech I made to the sergeant.

Then I found myself talking about my imprisonment in Germany. I don't know how it cropped up, but at all events it seemed perfectly natural at the time. The sergeant could not see the connection, but I kept telling him that, though the two incidents were separated by twenty years, there was no difference between them really. But how does one explain to a police sergeant that two things are really the same, and that something that happens later may be the cause of something that happened earlier, or *vice versa*? Though the latter alternative is something that anyone can understand. Meanwhile a hue and cry for my clothes was in progress. Why had they not been found in the woman's house? Had I entered it naked, or had I not? My trousers were found under the railway bridge, my shirt came to light round a fountain at Borghetto, a stone-breakers' village a quarter of a mile from the bridge, and my vest and pants were actually being worn by someone, one of those men who wander up and down the river looking for one thing and another. They identified him because they found his vest and pants in the pigsty at the woman's house. The sergeant arrested him, and among other things discovered that it was he who had crept into her bed because, he said, he had felt cold. This raised a whole new set of questions about me. Who had stripped me of my clothes? Who had beaten me up? The sergeant was so bewildered that he started a search for my shoes. He had found everything else but, so long as there was something he had not found, there was hope of discovering a clue that would clear up the whole mystery. They brought me about twenty shoes to look at.

It is incredible how full the world is of old shoes. But mine did not turn up, in spite of the admirable description of them I gave, I said they were worn out and curled up like a cabbage. This description resulted in the sergeant doing the cleverest thing he had ever done in his life. He arrived one evening with a cabbage, which he put on my bed. This made me bring up the whole story of my imprisonment in Germany. I even remember how I began. 'Talking of cabbages,' I said, and from there I went on right to the end. And then he understood, or seemed to understand. He linked my crossing the river naked twenty years before with my being found naked in the riverbed now, and at last he was able to jump those twenty years. But the conclusion he drew was a cheap and easy one. He said that I must have stripped this time too, and that I must have hurt myself falling from a height. That's all he could think of. Then we looked at each other in silence. And that was the end of the story. That morning there was an autumn-like dawn, ushered in by a great buzzing of flies. I felt homesick for Milan.

If I pretend to smoke,
for instance,
I drop ash on myself.

A line of blue neon light ran along the black wall, stained my face blue, and then zigzagged down to the wet street. Other lines of other colors also ran down the wall and ended up in the street. Also there was a word in lemon yellow, and there were some more letters, reflections of car lamps in the roadway, and illuminated shop window displays. I knew my face was blue, and I felt fine, because a graphic designer is in his element in a night townscape. The streets consist of numbers and letters, advertisement boards, and no entry and no waiting signs. So anyone like me who had just had an experience like mine could not help feeling fine with a blue face after the windows and shapes of the big buildings had disappeared. I had been back in Milan for several days, and often went out at night. I used to hang about on the pavement like the prostitutes, and sometimes I would talk to people with blue or red faces, and that at least was a novelty.

One evening a girl stopped beside me. My face at the time was orange, because that was the color it was painted by a big P in neon lighting that was hanging somewhere or other, and her face was of course orange too. My first feeling was that she had aged slightly. Aged as compared with the last time I had seen her? But as I had never seen her before, how could that be possible? We waited there for an hour without speaking. But somebody always ends by saying something, and actually it was she who spoke first, because I had nothing to say. She said she was waiting for someone. She had been waiting for him for a whole year. For a whole year? Yes, for a whole year. The last time she had seen him they had arranged to meet again at this spot, but he had failed to turn up. He had vanished. Vanished from Milan. Among other things, they had been going to get married, and she had got the flat and the furniture and everything ready. She had to. You never knew. You never knew what? She did not answer that question. Any of the yellow or blue faces that passed by might have belonged to the man she was waiting for. However, they did not.

On the fourth evening I insisted on going to see her flat, because words are one thing, after all, and facts are another. In short, I wanted to find out whether or not she was confusing the two.   I took her in the Volkswagen to the new quarter where she lived. It was in the Viale Zara district, as a matter of fact, but farther to the left.   There were six identical big six-story buildings, exactly like the six buildings on the other side of the city where I lived with my wife. Actually they had been planned by the same architect. He had put six in one place and six in another to void creating an excessively big and monotonous mass.   As it was, however, six formed an agreeable and harmonious little plateau. We went up to Emma's flat (she told her her

110

name in the car). It was on the same floor as ours, and the flat was just like ours too. In fact they were as similar as drops of water, except that we lived in the east of the city and she lived in the south. The furniture was covered with newspapers to protect them from dust. She ate in the kitchen, but everything else was covered with newspapers. She made me sit in a revolving chair, by Zanotta Poltrone of Lissone, catalogue No. 185. I told her I had one exactly like it. She wanted to take away the newspapers that covered the rest of the furniture, but I asked her to leave it as it was, otherwise she would only have to cover it all up again afterwards to prevent it from wearing out. After that events precipitated themselves in a most confusing manner. I don't know whether it was I who suggested she should sit on my knee, or whether the initiative came form her. At all events, after a minimum of brief phrases and little gestures, amounting to nothing at all in fact, we ended up by making love on the revolving chair. And I must say that it was most agreeable, perhaps because she had previously used this model 185 for the same purpose, and so knew what to do and how to move about on the tips of her toes to make it pivot and thus increase the sensation.

So we ended by seeing each other nearly every day, and our conversation always ended in our sitting on the model 185. When I sat on it, of course, she stoped talking and made the usual movements that led to the dizzy climax. Ultimately we got so used to each other that we began taking away the newspapers that covered the rest of the furniture. Then I notice that Emma had chosen furniture exactly similar to mine. Or perhaps the architect had suggested it; it is very easy for architects and graphic designers to share the same tastes, or rather for their tastes to be influenced by reading the same technical journals. Nearly all the furniture was white, and the cushions were a bright orange, some of them with purple lines. Even the arrangement of the furniture was the same, but that was more readily explicable, because the layout of the flat, and the few corners did not permit much variation. The consequence was that when all the furniture was uncovered I suddenly had the feeling I was at home. But for Emma's presence, I should have said I was at home. I am exaggerating, of course. Apart from anything else, the view from the windows made a big difference between the two flats. Here the surrounding houses were lower, and in particular there was a big detergent hoarding, while at home there was the long Corso Lodi and the Bitter Campari advertisement. However, whenever I sat down and Emma went out for a moment, to fetch a glass of water or something, I immediately had the feeling of not being sure where I was. To get rid of it I would get up and go over to the window, where the view set my doubts at rest.

But things began to get difficult at dusk, and between nine o'clock and midnight they grew worse. Especially if I were at home and in bed with my wife. In the dark I simply did not know whether I was in Emma's flat or my own. Among other things, as I often slept at Emma's - my excuse was having to work at night in my studio - there was hardly any way of telling whether the woman beside me was my wife or my mistress. This made me feel as queasy as a man off his balance. Of course I tried listening to the way the two women breathed, trying to spot any little differences, but they both slept in exactly the same way. Also they had exactly the same way of asking for something in the dark, in the same sleepy voice. But this made me cunning; I always turned on the light before answering, and so managed to shake off the nightmare. Also I got in the habit of talking very cautiously, so much so that one day I actually found myself stammering. Stammering of course is a familiar symptom of insecurity.

One evening I left Emma's flat, it must have been at about nine o'clock, drove across the city in the Volkswagen, and reached home at about 9.30. I opened the door, and there was Emma again, smiling and saying that dinner was ready. For a fraction of a second I felt I must have been absent-minded and made a stupid mistake - driven a few hundred yards or even half a mile or so and mechanically taken a wrong turning at the Piazza della Repubblica and find oneself going east instead of south, or the other way about. There was, however, a consideration that settled the matter. I had already had dinner with Emma, so it was inconceivable that she should have cooked me another. Though I was absolutely certain I had dined with her, and remembered exactly what we had talked about, as well as such details as how I had eaten the soup, that is, how she had fed me with it, putting spoonful after spoonful in my mouth, I wondered whether after all it might have been my wife with whom I had dined. But, apart from the inherent absurdity of the proposition, there was an obvious and incontrovertible fact that immediately and totally demolished it. The flat in which I was now was mine, as was clear from the big Bitter Campari advertisement that stood out in the night and the long, illuminated Corsi Lodi below. There could be no argument about that. So what was Emma doing here? She was behaving as if she was completely at home, as if she had always been here. I sat down at the table in front of the plate of soup, and as usual she started feeding me with the soup spoon. I ate with appetite, just as if I had not dined half an hour earlier. Perhaps I was remembering last night's meal. But I was satisfied in my own mind that half an hour earlier I had had spaghetti and bean soup.

On the other hand, I am not a bigot who believes he is always right. If Emma no lived in the flat in which I was, it meant that my flat was the other one. In other words, I lived in south Milan, not east. This was as sure as two and two make four, though some maintain that they can make three or even five. But basically I'm a traditionalist.

So I finished the meal, got up, and said goodnight to Emma, and went home in the Volkswagen. When I got there Luisa was looking at the television. I stayed with her for some time in silence. Then, more out of curiosity than anything else, I asked her what we had had for dinner that evening. 'Spaghetti and bean soup,' she said absent-mindedly. This revived my suspicions, and I remembered a feature of the bedroom ceiling, a small crack that while I was lying in bed one night before turning out the light had definitely assured me that I was at home and not at Emma's. I made some excuse not to go into the bedroom, switched on the light, and looked at the ceiling. The crack was not there. It might have been repaired. But when? I had a frantic desire to go to the other flat and examine the bedroom ceiling. I said that I had left some papers at my studio, and went out. Again I drove across the city in the Volkswagen. I got out on the sixth floor and went into the flat where I had left Emma about an hour previously. It was dark and silent. I assumed Emma had gone to bed. I went down the corridor, quietly opened the bedroom door, and switched on the light. Emma was asleep with her back towards me. I examined the ceiling, and discovered a small crack in the left-hand corner. I was just going to turn out the light again when Emma turned towards me. But it was not Emma. It was my wife. She asked me why on earth

I was so late. I sat on the bed with my back to her without answering. I did not ask myself any more questions, but began to undress. I firmly told myself to keep calm. I might simply have imagined the whole thing. I imagine a great many things while I am driving. Perhaps I had driven across Milan only once. Perhaps I had dined only once. I had just left Emma, and had now arrived at home for the first time that evening. I finished undressing, crept into bed, and turned out the light. I tried to go to sleep and eventually dropped off.

I never have time,
for instance,
to answer the letters you are going to write me.

I came and went between one flat and the other. But my
life was not limited to that alone. I also went back to
thinking about the lettering I had to devise, and I must
say that all the confusion surrounding me, the confusion
of my life with those two women, helped me to hit upon
the type of lettering I needed for Snaidero Sectional
Kitchens. I decided to reject the principle of clarity.
Immediacy of impact repelled me, and I had the feeling
that the man in the street, the public, was beginning to
share my feeling in the matter and turn away from it.
Nowadays everything was read so quickly that nothing
remained in the mind. So what was required was
something to break the rhythm, to slow down the pace
instead of accelerating it. Something that was
confusing, with more *entropy* and less *beat*. A
mysterious lettering, difficult to understand, like life,
forcing you to wonder what it was and what it meant.
When you had finally succeeded in reading the message
after five minutes, you would yourself in a way
contributed to the formation of the letters and words.
My first idea was not to use separate letters at all. I
started designing composite letters of those that share
the same stem. The result of superimposing a P and an
L on an I, for instance, is a character with the loop of the
P at the top and the foot of the L at the bottom. It's like

taking a man and putting his wife on top of him, plus his mistress, memories, friends, etc. In fact, it's precisely the same thing. Men go about with the imprints of their wives and all the rest of it upon them. That was what my lettering was like. I was the I, my wife was the P, and Emma was the L. One on top of the other. Confusion. An incomprehensible symbol bound sooner or later to yield its riddle, because clarity always underlay confusion, though you had to make an effort to find it. That was what I had to do in relation to my life, and what the public would have to do to decipher the advertiser's message. It was time for a mental effort to be demanded of people before their brains became atrophied by non-use. I began writing down first words and then ideas, condensing letters into one another, each idea being represented by different piles of superimposed letters. Each word had a striking attractiveness, with an element of mystery about it, rather like a Persian or Japanese script. They were condensed symbols that got into your blood and haunted you until they expanded in your mind, revealing the content of the message. That was the theory. It was an anti-clarity, anti-easy reading, anti-speed, anti-the-whole-of-modern-life theory. Yet at the same time, it was so modern in its conception. Words like men, having a past and a future, but above all having mystery. Nevertheless I was not yet completely satisfied. So I resorted to my scissors. I cut up vertically all the letters of the alphabet. I fragmented them. With the fragments

I started writing words, leaving a great deal of space between the fragments. The words seemed to vibrate as under a neon light. Also I noticed that fragments of one letter could be used for others. The stem, for instance. All the letters of the alphabet, with the single exception of V, could be built up with ten fragments only. V was the only weak point. Among other things, there emerged a radical and brilliant solution to my problem of designing lettering for the house emblem of a manufacturer of sectional kitchens. All that was needed was to write the firm's name in this fragmented alphabet. There would be no need to emphasize the initial S in Snaidero as Pirelli had done with its lengthened initial P, which gives such an excellent idea of elasticity, thus reminding us of its tires.

I telephoned Signor Snaidero at his works in Friuli.

Myself. - I have an exciting idea for the lettering of your trademark. Fragmented, sectionalized letters that can be put together like your kitchens.

He. - Is it easy to read?

Myself. - On the contrary, it's very difficult. That's where the novelty comes in. You grasp it a minute or so afterwards. But once you have grasped it, you remember it for the rest of your life.

He. - But... What about the women?... They find it hard enough to read ordinary script, and...

Myself. - Don't worry. Women will learn to use their brains.

He. - But they haven't got any.

Myself. - They have, I assure you. Don't worry about that.

He. - I was thinking of having strips seventy-five yards long in football stadiums. What do you think of that?

Myself. - An excellent idea.

He. - (After a long silence). The only thing is that in a football stadium spectators are continually moving their heads, following the ball. How can they take in a message if they don't understand it?

Myself. - The spectators at a football match are men. Kitchens are bought by women.

He. - (Another silence). But, as I said, women don't read.

Myself. - All the better. What matters is that they will assimilate the message in their bellies. The message will explode in their minds later, at home or in the tram. It will be a kind of indirect publicity, as it were. We've had enough of clarity. Clarity in words and clarity in life. More than enough.

On one of those days, actually it was one evening, I compiled a detailed diary of my future life. I was leaning against the marble of a cathedral, looking at the big mobile writing on the facade of the building opposite. I was not reading the advertising message, but the diary of my future life. I partly read it and partly thought it.

I was going to live in an abandoned car, parked by the pavement in the city outskirts. It might be an Italian car, or it might be a foreign car. Actually, when I came to consider the matter, I felt sure it would be my own Volkswagen. When it was reduced to a wreck, with the tires flat and the upholstery in shreds, I should abandon it by the pavement in the outer suburbs. Then, when I was reduced to being a vagrant with no fixed abode, neither my wife's nor my mistress's, I should go and look for it, and when I found it I should settle down inside it. At night I should sleep on the backseat covered with newspapers, and in the daytime, when I didn't want to go out, I should sit in the front seat, looking through the dusty windscreen. I should rest my elbows on the steering wheel, stretch out as if I was lying on a couch, and look at the accelerator, the brake and the clutch. And when spring came I should lower the windows and let in the sunshine. During the summer I should cover the windows with yellow paper and stay in the shade.

When the police came and wanted to know to whom the car belonged, I should tell them that it was mine. When they told me to remove it because it was causing an obstruction, I should point out that it was my home. Then they would come with a breakdown van and tow it away somewhere, but I should refuse to get out. I should tell them that it was my home and that I intended to stay in it, and they wouldn't know what to do. And so the story would get into the newspapers. A

123

few people would get very indignant and tell me off, but then the excitement would die down and I should be left in peace.

I should have no more trouble with women, work, clothes, baths, the heat or the cold, keeping fit, shaving, having my hair cut, or paying bills. Until all the peace and quiet got on my nerves and caused another crisis which I should be unable to explain. It would be something like the revolt against the easy life that can so often be observed among vagrants. I should despise myself for having cast off all ties. I should go about kicking stones, until one day I stopped at the edge of a big hole full of old tin cans. I should start talking to the other tramps and vagrants at the edge of the hole. Though perhaps I might not talk to them, but just go to sleep on the tin cans, which would slide down to the bottom of the hole, taking me with them, whereupon the other vagrants would try to bury me underneath them. But I should defend myself by flinging tins at them and manage to scramble out. They would try to kick back again, but I should bite their feet, and one of the wretches would start yelling that I had eaten his big toe. But it wouldn't be true, I should only have hurt it. Then the excitement would die down, and I should sit down at the edge of the hole. One of them, a criminal type, would want to sleep with his head on my shoulders, but I wouldn't let him, and he would go to sleep lying on my legs. Because of this I should be unable to move. Then I should begin, etc. etc. etc.

There are people who don't know where to go,
for instance,
but are in a great hurry to get there.

I don't know who it was who first pointed out that in the last resort one always falls in love with the same woman. At all events I'm in a better position than anyone else to corroborate it, for one thing because of my belief that everyone always falls in love with himself. There's always something in common with two women with whom one falls in love, either in their ways or in their character or particularity of their appearance. I had immediately noticed that Emma and Luisa were alike in a number of ways: the forehead, more or less the same physique, the same smile. True, there were other things in which they were completely different. It was only for fleeting moments that Luisa reminded me of Emma, or *vice versa,* but they always gave me a feeling of bewilderment, whereupon whichever one of them it was would invariably ask me what I was thinking about. All women always ask that question when they notice whoever they happen to be talking to looks a bit *distrait*, and sometimes men do too. I believe I am correct in stating that at such times the individual concerned is really thinking about someone else who his companion has reminded him of; or perhaps about someone whom he cannot remember but saw somewhere or other though he cannot remember where. All he has is a vague feeling about it. My situation was different. When I spoke to Emma I could see Luisa in her, and thus I had a real point of reference; and it was the same the other way about...

If that had been all, if it had been just a matter of moments of distraction only, it would have been too trifling to bother about, but in fact the situation gradually grew more complicated. Luisa and Emma grew more and more alike. An infinity of changes are of course brought about as a result of seeing the same advertisements - hair style, clothes, deodorants, eye color, and so forth. This applies particularly to readers of the same women's journals, and both women read the same magazines, and both subscribed to *Grazia* and other publications of the same type, including *Elle*. Luisa and Emma, in short, were subject to the same publicity influences. Even their underclothes were identical. They ended up differing only in the shape of their ears, nose, and eyes. Luisa's eyes were more almond-shaped. However, not only did the differences become minimal, but those that remained were increasingly obliterated, because sometimes they wore their hair over their ears, thus concealing one of the basic clues for distinguishing between them, and Emma often used a black pencil to change the shape of her eyes, thus depriving Luisa of an exclusive characteristic.

One day I actually started believing that the two were in league. They must be seeing each other, going to the same hairdresser, the same dressmaker and the same shops, cooperating with each other in

128

exchanging flats, conspiring behind my back to drive me mad. No other conclusion was possible. I was quivering on the brink of utter chaos. I no longer knew which was my mistress and which was my wife. I had probably, or rather certainly, resumed having sexual relations with Luisa, and her reactions were of course exactly the same as Emma's. She too liked intercourse on Zanotta Poltrone of Lissone's revolving chair model 185, and there was the same giddy whirl at the culminating moment. I had given up talking. I no longer cared whether it was the detergent advertisement or the Bitter Campari hoarding that was outside the window. Where I was, I was. Actually I had the sensation of no longer being anywhere, of being provisionally situated wherever I was. I had the feeling that my feet were no longer on the ground.

Also, and this I would not care to explain, not only did the two start getting more and more alike, but other women whom I saw in bars, or caught sight of, say, at the wheel of a car held up at the traffic lights, would remind me in some way of my wife and Emma. The miniskirts may have had something to do with it, and also the heavy eye make-up. So it was not only at home that I was faced with this confusion; it was just the same when I was out, as if Milan were populated with identical women. However, when I was out I generally managed. A glance, or sometimes a brief pursuit, either on foot or in the car, was sufficient for me to establish that it was a different woman. But that was not always the case. One evening I followed Emma when she came out of a bar and walked towards a car parked near the newspaper seller in the Piazza San Babila. I crept along close to the wall until I got to the car, put a cigarette in my mouth and struck a match in order to catch a glimpse of the young man at the wheel. He was a young man of about thirty. He may have been the architect, or another of her lovers. I was seized withe jealousy, took her arm to prevent her from getting in, she slapped my face, the young man got out and seized me by my coat collar, and a heated altercation followed. The woman intervened and said her name was Monica, and in fact her voice was different from Emma's. So I apologized, and made up some excuse to explain the mistake. I walked off, swearing to take no more interest in any of the women who reminded me of Emma or my wife, either in the street or anywhere else.

I had more than enough to occupy my mind in what was going on in the two flats, where things were getting more involved than ever. One afternoon I had the feeling that both women were in the flat, whichever flat it was. They did not appear at the same time, of course, or I should have laid my cards on the table and had it out with them. The sort of thing that happened was this. Luisa would get up from the dinner table for some reason and go into the next room for a moment, but it was not she who reappeared, but Emma, who came in and sat down and went on with the meal, taking up the conversation at the point where Luisa dropped it.

Or it would be the other way about. I would be in bed
with Emma, and she would get up to fetch a glass of
water. But it would be Luisa who came back with it, of
course wearing the same pyjamas and the same hair-
curlers.

I pretended to notice nothing, because I could
not be 100 percent sure of my facts. If I had been, I
should have played quite a different tune. I just awaited
my opportunity, even pretending to be more and more
bewildered and confused, to encourage them to carry on
their little game more audaciously. Of course it was
possible that one or both of them liked this *ménage à
trois*, but lacked the courage to admit it openly. There
are plenty of relationships of that kind in Milan. Two
men and a woman, or two women and a man, and of
course other and greater complications that result from
trying to preserve a facade of happy married life before
the final breach. Had it perhaps been some proposal of
this kind that Luisa had left unspoken when we talked
through the cane fence?

The occasion I was waiting for at last arrived.
One day, when I realized that both women were in the
flat, Luisa rose from the table to go and fetch toothpicks.
I covered her soup plate before Emma had time to come
in, and it was obvious that she was disconcerted. She
did not know whether to finish the soup or go on to the
next course. Before she had time to say anything, I got
up and said I had to go out. I took the Volkswagen and

dashed to the other flat before Luisa could get there. This time I was going to surprise her.

I crossed the city in a flash, went up in the lift, and opened the flat door. Or rather tried to open it, because the key would not turn in the lock. But then the door was opened a few inches from the inside, enough to enable me to see a man in pyjamas. I could see only a part of him, but there was no doubt about it, that man was me. The eyes with which he looked at me were mine, and so was his chin, and so was his forehead. The fact that I could not see the whole of him was immaterial. After seeing yourself in a mirror every day for forty years, you don't need a great deal to be able to recognize yourself.

'Yes?'

I could not answer. I was so utterly taken aback that I could not answer. Meanwhile those eyes looked at me without any particular surprise.

'Yes? What is it you want?'

I did not know what to say to myself. Actually, of course, if that man were me I had a thousand questions to put to him, there were a thousand problems to solve. Too many.

Eventually I managed to answer.

'You tell me first,' I said.

I waited anxiously for him to say something, but he did not speak. He too had the impression that I was confused. Slowly he closed the door, leaving me with my eyes glued to the dark wood.

I walked down one step at a time. I don't know why it did not occur to me to use the lift as I always did. Perhaps I wanted to think. In my bewilderment I looked for the Volkswagen, but could not find it. There were two Fiats and a Citroen. Perhaps in my hurry I had come by taxi, but I was not sure. I crossed the courtyard and walked slowly in the direction of the city centre without realizing that I was walking. Meeting someone who was my spit image was an experience of another world. The strangest thing about it was that he hadn't shown the slightest sign of surprise at the sight of someone who was as much like him as two peas in a pod. As a token of goodwill, however, I assumed I was someone else. A graphic designer, but a different one. But who was I? Walking along with lowered head, my attention was attracted more than once by things such as sheets of newspaper, cigarette ends, and even matchboxes. The streets are full of things that people throw away, apparently useless rubbish that I wanted to pick up. The feeling came to me quite naturally. What was behind that desire of my hands to pick up things, and of my eyes to scan the streets? Was it perhaps an ancient pattern of hereditary gestures dating from past experience? However, it reassured me, because it meant that it was I who had been in the house in the country and the concentration camp in Germany. I and not that other man. It was I who had walked about in the ashes looking for things and had later developed a passionate interest in stones and matchboxes. So I was a single person, and not two. If I had been someone else, I should have had different ways and different compulsions. This made me feel better. At all events, I did not bend down and pick up anything, for one thing because the pavement was full of shoes walking past all the little things that attracted me. Men's shoes, women's shoes, children's shoes. Shoes that passed by indifferently, sometimes actually crushing the bits of rubbish I wanted to collect. I had no desire to take a tram, or a taxi, or even to talk to the passersby, so I tried to avoid even glancing at them. Or perhaps it was they who desired to have no contact with me. In short, it practically amounted to mutual contempt. Eventually, however, I decided to take a tram, and I felt in my pockets to make sure I had some money. But I had none, a things that can happen to anyone, but, particularly, to the absent-minded. I know a man who never has a pocket handkerchief when he wants to blow his nose, though his wife invariably put one in his pocket before he goes out. Actually he works as a librarian in the Vatican. No, he used to be a librarian, heaven knows what he's doing nowadays. As I was saying, finding oneself in the street without any money in one's pocket is a thing that can happen to anyone, but I did find in my pocket a damp, chewed, rusty-looking apple core. I tried to think who could have played me such a trick. It must have been in my pocket for heaven knows how long, or perhaps I had picked it up without meaning to, imagining it to be heaven knows what. It must have been an automatic action, like putting your foot on the clutch when changing gear, you don't realize you're doing it, because your foot moves of its own accord. Obviously I had picked up this apple core the same way. I dropped it among the people waiting for the tram and walked away. Just because going out without a penny in one's pocket is a thing that can happen to anybody, I dislike asking a stranger for 50 or 100 lire, even though I am sure he would willingly give it to me.

I walked along, keeping close to the walls in order to get along as quickly as possible. I walked two or three miles like that, I must say entirely effortlessly, as if I had been in training for long walks. It was exhilarating, and gave me the feeling I was still in full physical health. I felt young. Sometimes I lengthened my stride and raised my elbows, as long distance walkers do. I saw someone on television walking like that, an Abyssinian I think, the one who won the marathon at the Olympic Games in Rome. I leant forward slightly to assume a more aerodynamic posture. I actually had the feeling I was running. At one point I began running, because I could see the outline of a stadium ahead, and I wanted to finish with a burst of speed. It was a pity I had no way of timing myself, but I did not have my watch with me. But I counted the seconds in my head. So far I had taken twenty-eight minutes. To calculate my speed I decided immediately to cover the same ground again in the Volkswagen. I reached the block of flats in which I live, counting the seconds aloud. I went through the glass door shouting twenty-three. So I had taken twenty-eight minutes, twenty-three seconds. I was panting when I entered the lift and made as if to press the button for the sixth floor, but there were only five floors. The sixth had gone. Hurriedly I emerged from the lift, assuming I had entered the wrong building by mistake. There are several of them all alike, and when one is in a hurry it's easy to enter the wrong one. I went into the lifts of all five neighboring buildings, and there was no doubt there were only five floors in each. I went outside again, and looked at the six buildings from some distance away. Only now did I begin to suspect that I had come to the wrong district. The color of the windows seemed to be different, these were lighter, and perhaps their shape was different too. While I was about it, I had a look at the parked cars, naturally looking for my mouse-colored Volkswagen, but it was not there. Or rather there was a red Volkswagen surrounded by a swarm of Fiats. I wondered whether my Volkswagen were mouse-colored or red. I might have painted it, or my wife or even my mistress might have done so. So I looked to see whether there was anything inside that belonged to me, the little white rabbit, for instance, tied to the inside mirror. No, in this Volkswagen there was a black rabbit, and on the shelf between the backseat and the rear window there was a book of comicstrips with pages curled by the sun. So it could not have been my

Volkswagen, not so much because of the black rabbit as because of the comicstrips. I never look at comicstrips. Never. Nor do my wife or mistress. The first thing I do before establishing relations with a woman is to ask her whether she looks at comicstrips. If she says yes, I clear off.

I walked away from the six buildings, looking for the nearest shopping street. Of course I was feeling rather bewildered. I stopped still on the pavement to review the situation, concentrating intensely. I admit that I was very bewildered indeed. Then I walked on again, unhurriedly. Then I stopped, to look at a cigarette butt that someone had thrown away. It was still burning, and the smoke rose in spirals to where I was standing. I made some reflections about spirals before walking on again.

The most incredible thing happened while I was standing in front of a shop window. Actually I had my back to it, and as usual was standing with bent head, looking at a heap of rubbish with some fish bones in the middle of it. I raised my head just when a distinguished looking man of about fifty passed by. He stopped, and put something in my hand. It was fifty lire. It was a mistake, of course. Perhaps I had raised my hand to point at something, or it may simply have been a gesture accompanying some thought of mine, and he must have thought that I was begging, and stopped and put fifty lire in my palm. A trivial incident, deserving no more than a smile. In fact I laughed aloud. But, as other people were passing right in front of me and I did not want them to think I was standing in the street laughing at nothing, I turned and faced the window and went on laughing. It was a tall and very modern window, with aluminium corners, and inside there was a random pile of old tennis shoes. There were all sorts, big, little, some with colored stripes, some without laces, some with holes in the toe. It was the first time I had ever seen a shop window full of old tennis shoes. Heaven knows who bought them. However, if people bought them, they also wore them, and so I looked at them. Then there was a sudden reflection of something in the window, it may have been a passing car or a bus, but whatever it was the glass at the height of my face became opaque, a kind of shadow disturbed its transparency, and it was then that I saw my own reflection. At first I thought the face in the glass was someone else's. It had a long beard, and its owner was dirty and in tatters, and I did not believe that the reflection was mine. I touched my face and my clothes and, sure enough, my beard was an inch long, and I really was like what I saw. Why had I not realized it sooner? It's easy to talk at random. One might talk for half an hour, explaining that not seeing or feeling oneself is a thing that might happen to anyone. One might say tat it's perfectly possible to see oneself in the mirror or feel oneself without noticing anything because, quite apart from distraction, one generally sees oneself or feels oneself automatically, just as one puts one's foot on the clutch automatically as I mentioned before.

I wondered whether to go and see some friend. But even this idea was disturbing, because the name's of friends I remembered and the faces I connected with them were different from what I expected. I recognized certain features of those faces - noses, ears, spectacles, for instance - but all the rest belonged to people I had never seen. Or perhaps I had seen them, and it was those noses or ears or spectacles that threw everything into confusion. With names it was the same. I no longer felt sure that my friends' names were what I believed them to be at that moment. However, friends or no friends, I needed to talk to someone, to unburden myself, to hand over the baffling maze of my situation to someone else, to have it sorted out for me. So I started examining all of the passersby, hoping to see the right face, in short, the face of a person who could be accosted there and then and had at least an hour to spare to listen to a stranger's story. The young could not possibly understand a problem like mine so I dismissed them out of hand. I needed someone of at least thirty, whether a man or a woman was immaterial. Such a person was by no means easy to find, particularly at this time of day when everyone was in a hurry. I caught glimpses of faces in profile, and persons holding their heads high because they knew where they were going and as if the better to cleave the air. However, at last I spotted a working man, aged about thirty, strolling along on the other side of the street and stopping every now and then to glance at the shop windows. I followed him. I started looking at the shop windows too, waiting for the right moment to engage him in conversation. Then he turned down a side street. I caught up with him and walked just behind him, determined to stop him at the first opportunity, but just when I had made up my mind to talk to him he vanished into a doorway. There was nothing for it but to walk straight on. I was in a working-class district. I remembered the country police sergeant. I needed someone with his patience now. I had told him any amount of things including what had happened in Germany. So I made up my mind to apply to a Carabinieri barracks. But, as my habit of looking at street signs and all the scribbling on the walls never left me (again corroborating that it was I and not the other man who was the graphic designer), I noticed a big triangle and three little ones chalked beside the door of a house. For the benefit of the uninformed, this is a beggars' and vagabonds' sign. It means 'sob story needed here', i.e. the occupants of this house are compassionate and willing to listen, and if you want alms from them you must spin them a yarn about having a large family of hungry children. There are any number of such signs. A three-toothed comb, for instance, means 'beware of the dog', a circle with a point inside it means here the people are alright, and a circle with an arrow right across it tells you not to waste your time but to go away and try somewhere else.

I knew these things, not because I had inexplicably been reduced to a state of mendicancy, but because I had made a small study of the subject in America when I went there to attend Gropius's lectures. Actually I had connected those signs with those drawn on the pavements outside blocks of flats by itinerant saleswomen who call at people's homes selling detergents and that sort of thing.

Anyhow, I walked into the house and found myself facing a woman of about sixty, sitting behind a desk and fidgeting with a silver ashtray. She looked at me as if she had been expecting me, and pointed to a chair beside the door, no doubt the chair on which all her callers sat. I felt at ease immediately. I started telling her everything from the beginning, quietly and calmly and without leaving anything out. She looked at me with greater and greater amusement, as if she were enjoying my story, and I realized or rather assumed that she was lonely or desperate and did not know what to do to pass the time. So I went on talking, saying things at random just for the sake of talking. I don't know how it happened, but I ended up talking about silver. Perhaps it was because of the ashtray she kept turning over and over in her hands for no conceivable reason. I showed her the marks on the silver, and explained their meaning. I explained that the small lion in a square field was a guarantee that it was silver, that the three towers stood for Exeter, which is a town in England, and that the letter of the alphabet indicated the year of manufacture, and I also told her a great many other things about silver. Then I grew tired and stopped talking. We stayed looking at each other without talking for quite a long time, I don't know how long. Perhaps she was waiting for me to go on. But I had had enough. I could not go on. Among other things, it was useless. I made as if to get up, and she handed me a piece of bread and one of those triangular pieces of Galbani cheese that are given to children. I put the stuff in my pocket and took my departure. But I did not feel desperate.

When things grow too complicated I lose all desire to solve them and stop asking myself questions. Yes, that was the thing to do. Stop talking and entrust oneself to one's body, one's arms, one's instinct, as the animals do. And indeed I felt better straight away. Even though the thoughts passing through my mind were in sharp conflict with what I was doing, I still went on picking up things. I moved along very quickly, with my eyes glued to the ground, particularly the gutter. Very few things are dropped in the middle of the roadway or, if they are, they are quickly driven back into the gutter by the wind or the wheels of passing cars. I stuffed all sorts of things into my pockets. Every so often I raised my eyes and looked at people. A multitude of faces displaying a paltry equilibrium in the light of the UPIM shop windows, a cascade of light that settled even on their ears. A multitude of mouths well able to say the words soap, toothpaste, even bath-salts. People with x-ray plates of their chest and pelvis in their pockets, complicated bone structures entirely devoid of adventure. Only the advertisements shrieked PERBORATO, TRISMACCHIA, WASHES WHITER, SUPER, OMO, OLA, KNORR. I wondered whether the whole of man, the whole of man... Other thoughts came... his shouting at the lions, his love of the clouds... But instead the body is thrown away like cigarette stubs, or arms when windows are broken. But what can one do, what can one do, what can one do? I wondered what day of the week it was. They were like wardrobes, wardrobes with a hornet inside, no traces of ghosts or murderers. A city of wardrobes, wardrobes with drawers full of GARDOL to keep your breath sweet. What was needed was fire, or earthquake, or worse still. I walked on, keeping close to the wall, surrounded by people again. FOOTWARE end of season sale, CUTLER, SUSY, EVERYTHING FOR THE CHILDREN, LA PANTOFOLA, delivery to any part of the world, GIFT SHOP, huge assortment, TOBACCONISTS. I stopped to pick up a military uniform button. Then on again along the wall, still surrounded by people. Young people, clean young people with no desire to walk up the facades of the houses. All Italy was like this, day and night. Negroes with saxophones ought to be mingled with them, or Chinese or other races, and with them problems, even some religion or other. I don't know.

Towards the outskirts I started rummaging in the dustbins, and I helped myself to all the sheets of

143

newspaper I could find in them. Occasionally a whole newspaper was among them. I sat down at a table in a bar to fold them, as well as some brown paper I had found, into four. Like that they took up less space. But the waiter came over, took me by the arm and threw me out because, he said, I was dirtying the tables. He also used some filthy expressions. But I did not seem to hear. I saw a mouth opening, but ignored what it said. Then when I walked on and thought about the way his mouth moved I imagined that he might well have been using filthy expressions at me.

I walked quickly, because I was tired and wanted to get home. There was something about the luminous signs scattered about that reminded me of some place that was familiar to me. But I was not sure that it was a house to which I was going. I had a feeling I was going towards a bridge, and under the bridge I vaguely remembered a kind of hut. Perhaps it was there that I was going. Heaven knew how many days, months, or even years I had been living in it. But it was also possible that the hut did not exist and that I simply slept under the bridge. No doubt the newspapers I had collected were to cover me up, to protect me against the cold and damp. But then a thought flashed through my mind. Or rather it was not so much a thought as an image. I saw my Volkswagen abandoned somewhere, the tires flat, the body dented, the upholstery in shreds. So it was in the Volkswagen that I slept? It seemed to be so.

Across the road I caught a glimpse of faces that were illuminated when a match was struck, the faces of people bearing the marks of a balanced, provincial poverty, and also some hungry faces, but lacking the element of inner desperation, the cosmic squalor, to be found among the human wrecks of the Bowery in New York. In one way there was very little poison about, even in the air, there was a trace of smoke and that was all, with no additional poisons and no electricity. The pavements began to be irregular and full of holes, and so every now and then I stumbled. The ground now began speaking to me; its irregular surface mounted through my feet and shaped itself in my head. That, incidentally, is the Japanese theory. They like unsmooth gardens, so that the garden should speak to you through your feet and give you its physical feel as if it were a statue to be looked at with your feet. Here and there were low, dark houses, open windows, dark interiors with the television switched on. A western, with galloping horses, and some shots, some shots. Until the ground started trembling beneath my feet. Then I started hurrying across fields and ditches, and long, muddy expanses. I entered a wood, and even the branches of the trees were quivering. The firing grew more intense, shells whistled through the air, and I began to run. Several times I struck my head against tree-trunks. At the end of the wood I came to an open space illuminated by a windy dawn. Bits of paper were flying through the air and bullets whizzed by, but I walked through it all unworried and with my head high, as if I knew I was not going to be hit, though German soldiers were falling to the ground and crying out all round me. I stepped over blood-stained faces, and arms sticking into the ground and overturned lorries, looking for the sheep, and came to the place where they were munching grass in the ditch, guarded by the sheepdog that would not let them eat the corn. I sat down near the dog to see the sheep that wanted to be disobedient, and in fact the third sheep from the end stuck out its nose and tried to eat the corn, but the dog went for it and bit it before returning to sit by me. I got up and walked on through the smoke. I stumbled. I saw an arm passing, holding a bayonet. I reached a house, went in, walked upstairs and entered the room. The plates were on the table, full of soup, and I saw the silver cutlery and the place where I knew I must sit. Then the German airmen in their brown leather flying suits trooped in. They sat down, and I went on eating with them. This time we were friends. One of them should have slapped me on the back, but he forgot. So I went over to him and made sure he did slap me on the back. I hurried out of the house with them, and helped them to remove the camouflage nets from the aircraft, which then took off. The sergeant arrived with the motorcycle combination, and I jumped in the sidecar, without waiting for him to take hold of me by the collar and put me in. We drove through another wood and followed a variety of country roads until we got to the little concentration camp and went in. I saw the ashes, Violini, the Polish priest, the elephant man, the girl I was going to fall in love with, and everything else, including the crows. The commandant emerged from the villa with his cabbage. He began detaching the leaves with his hook and handing them out. With a smile on his face he ordered the prisoner who had stolen his watch to step forward. All the prisoners round me were quivering with fear. Not me I laughed. I knew I was going to come through though. I knew I was going to come through.

Tonino Guerra was born in Santarcangelo di Romagna, Italy. The son of illiterate peasants, Guerra first started writing poetry in his early twenties, while interned in a German prison camp with other anti-fascist protesters. After the war he moved to Rome where he met the director Elio Petri, an event that heralded the start of his screenwriting career. He went onto produce over one hundred film scripts, receiving Oscar nominations for Carlo Pointi's *Casanova 70*, and Michelangelo Antoninoi's *Blow-Up*. In 1975 he won the Academy Award for Fellini's *Amarcord*.

Michael Bracewell is the author of several works of fiction and non-fiction, including a novella *Perfect Tense* (1999) and *England Is Mine* (1997). His writing has also appeared in *The Faber Book of Pop* and T*he Penguin Book of Twentieth Century Fashion Writing*. Recent publications include *The Rise of David Bowie 1971-1972* (with Mick Rock and Barney Hoskyns) and *Joy Division* (with Glenn Brown and Lavinia Greenlaw). He is a contributor to The Burlington and Burlington Contemporary and was co-curator of *The Secret Public* (Kunstverein Munich/ICA, London (2006)) and *The Dark Monarch: British Modernism and the Occult* at Tate St Ives (2009). His selected writings on visual art, *The Space Between,* were published by Ridinghouse, London in 2011.

Eric Mosbacher was an English journalist and translator. During World War II he worked as an interpreter interrogating Italian prisoners of war before joining the Political Warfare Executive, where he helped to create an anti-Fascist German-language newspaper.